# SHAMAN STONE SOUP

# *Praise for* SHAMAN STONE SOUP

"I really enjoyed reading *Shaman Stone Soup*. It was clearly written from the heart, and facilitates understanding about shamanism and alternative spiritual paths, as well as helps people to believe in miracles. I appreciated how Herrera was able to follow the spiritual guidance she was receiving without fighting or questioning it. *Shaman Stone Soup* is a real example of what can be accomplished through the power of trust. And it also shows what is possible when we allow the helping spirits to bring through healing."

— SANDRA INGERMAN, Author of eight books, including *Soul Retrieval* and *Shamanic Journeying: A Beginner's Guide*

"Shaman Elizabeth Herrera proves that miracles surround us through charming verbal illustrations that resonate in the heart and soul. Unique and captivating, we need only to listen in order to learn her subtle, yet powerful spiritual message."

— SONIA VON MATT STODDARD,
*Awareness Magazine*

"*Shaman Stone Soup* is an inspiring and educational journey into the nature of shamanism, and through personal storytelling demonstrates how our connection with nature and each other helps dissolve our illusions of separation, allowing miracles to occur in our everyday lives."

— CINDY LORA-RENARD, New Age Singer and Song Writer, and Spiritual Counselor

"Take this journey into the world of the Shaman and the miraculous power of love in the healing process."

— LOUIS LaGRAND, Ph.D., CT Loss Education Associates, Author of *Love Lives On*

"*Shaman Stone Soup* offers a clear, down-to-earth perspective on the ancient practice of shamanic journeying, illustrating ways that it can support the innate healing capacities of body, mind and spirit. The author's beautifully written and heartfelt stories demonstrate the powers of compassion, caring and prayer when they are focused through ritual and journeying. This very personal memoir of Herrera's healing work makes the techniques of shamanic healing accessible to any interested reader, with valuable glimpses into the deep and universal spiritual roots of all healing processes."
— HAL Z. BENNETT, PH.D., Writing Coach and Best-Selling Author of over 30 books, including *Spirit Animals & The Wheel of Life* and *Writing Spiritual Books*

"Shaman Elizabeth has shared her experiences in a way that honors all the healing, revealing work that is done by urban shamans everywhere. The writing style invited me in and kept me present to the last page. An excellent read."
— REVEREND EMILE GAUVREAU, Center for Spiritual Living Cape Coral

"Elizabeth's beautifully written book, telling of her spiritual journey, is so much more than a memoir. It is also a guide book for those who have awakened, and for those who have yet to awaken, but are feeling the stirring of their own personal impending and inevitable wake-up call."
— JOY AYSCUE, Co-founder of The Conscious Healing Initiative

"A delightful and warm read. Instills peace in one's soul."
— MICHAEL WISOTZKE, Truth Seeker Forum

"*Shaman Stone Soup* offers a clear, down-to-earth perspective on the ancient practice of shamanic journeying, illustrating ways that it can support the innate healing capacities of body, mind and spirit. The author's beautifully written and heartfelt stories demonstrate the powers of compassion, caring and prayer when they are focused through ritual and journeying. This very personal memoir of Herrera's healing work makes the techniques of shamanic healing accessible to any interested reader, with valuable glimpses into the deep and universal spiritual roots of all healing processes."
— HAL Z. BENNETT, PH.D., Writing Coach and Best-Selling Author of over 30 books, including *Spirit Animals & The Wheel of Life* and *Writing Spiritual Books*

"Shaman Elizabeth has shared her experiences in a way that honors all the healing, revealing work that is done by urban shamans everywhere. The writing style invited me in and kept me present to the last page. An excellent read."
— REVEREND EMILE GAUVREAU, Center for Spiritual Living Cape Coral

"Elizabeth's beautifully written book, telling of her spiritual journey, is so much more than a memoir. It is also a guide book for those who have awakened, and for those who have yet to awaken, but are feeling the stirring of their own personal impending and inevitable wake-up call."
— JOY AYSCUE, Co-founder of The Conscious Healing Initiative

"A delightful and warm read. Instills peace in one's soul."
— MICHAEL WISOTZKE, Truth Seeker Forum

# THE PARABLE OF STONE SOUP

A poor man, who was hungry, walked into a village. Having no money, he found water in the center of the square and filled his only possession, an iron pot.

He then found a stone and put it into the water. He built a fire and waited for the water to simmer.

One of the villagers became curious and asked him what he was doing.

"I am making stone soup," the poor man replied.

The villager peered into the pot and saw a solitary stone resting on the bottom beneath the simmering water.

The poor man continued, "It just needs a wee bit of garnish to improve the flavor. Perhaps a carrot would help."

The villager did not mind parting with a small portion of what he had, so he gave one of his carrots to the poor man and it was added to the soup.

Other villagers approached and each gave a little of what they had.

More ingredients were added until it became a delicious and nourishing soup that was enjoyed by all.

# SHAMAN
# STONE SOUP

*True-life stories that show
miracles can happen to anyone!*

ELIZABETH M. HERRERA

**Inspirational true-life stories.** *Shaman Stone Soup* brings miracles to life through true-life stories of the author's personal experiences as a spiritual healer for friends, family and clients. You will read about the ghost who overstayed her welcome, the spirits of ancient wise men who offered advice and a miraculous cure from cancer for a friend, a conversation with a hurricane and its unintended impact, the man who got out of his wheelchair to go hunting and fishing, a vivid dream and later chance meeting of a pastor who needed guidance, the transformation of a schizophrenic, the loving afterlife contact from the author's mother who died unexpectedly, and many other stories.

*First edition, December 2010*
*Second edition, August 2016*

*The information contained in this book is not a substitute for medical or professional care, and you should not use the information in place of a visit, consultation, or the advice of your physician or other healthcare provider.*

*Portions of the names, locations, and other identifying information in these true-life stories have been changed to protect the privacy of the people involved. Fictitious names are indicated with quotation marks when first mentioned.*

# Acknowledgments

To my mother, Judy, who offered her enthusiasm
and encouragement. Whenever I doubted
my path as a healer, she prodded me on.

To my sister, Sharon, for being a part of
so many of the miracles in my life.

To my father, Bob, for introducing me to *A Course
in Miracles,* the inspiring conversations that we've
had over the years, and the insights he offered
that improved the stories within these pages.

To Janet Harvey-Clark for being a
wonderful editor and friend.

# In Gratitude

I offer my thanks to the Spirit,

through whom all things are possible,

the spirit guides for their patience,

my power animals for offering their

guidance and archetype power,

each client that has allowed me to be

a part of their healing process,

Jesus for showing us the way, and

God for being a loving creator.

# CONTENTS

*Dedicated to my mother who passed*

*away during the writing of this book.*

*Although she was a devoted Christian,*

*she supported me as I followed a*

*spiritual path outside of religion.*

*She once said, "All healing comes from God."*

*It was a gentle reminder that the form is*

*never more important than the spirit.*

*She is missed.*

# Memoir — The Path to Miracles

"You must learn from the mistakes of others. You can't possibly live long enough to make them all yourself."

— Samuel Levenson

I never thought I would be a healer, much less a shaman. I enjoyed a successful life as a graphic designer and owner of a small design firm—and the perks that went along with it. But it seemed the Spirit had other plans for me.

In my early 20s, I lost my faith, and its absence left a hole in my heart that I didn't know how to fill. My faith had always been important to me, which is why I was surprised that I would lose it because of the profound impact of a single book, *The Great Cosmic Mother: Rediscovering the Religion of the Earth* by Monica Sjöö and Barbara Mor. The book explored the religious traditions and cultures of humanity since the earliest known worship of the Goddess and Mother Earth.

After reading the book, I had a much better understanding of the tragic impact of patriarchal religions throughout history and came to believe that too much of what my religion had proclaimed was a lie. I further rationalized that if religion was a lie, then so was God. I was too young to see that religion and God did not have to go hand-in-hand and, subsequently, lost my faith in both.

However, my life began to change again in 2002 when I read the bestselling book *The Four Agreements* by Don Miquel Ruiz. In the book, Ruiz mentioned that he was a shaman, a medicine man, as was his mother and ancestors. Being of Hispanic and Native American descent, shamanism intrigued me. I thought perhaps it was a Mexican religion I had never heard of and vowed that if I ever got the chance to learn more about it, I would.

A few months later, I received a newsletter from a local hospital offering a workshop on shamanism, in addition to their usual classes on diabetes, high-blood pressure and healthy living. Although a hospital-sponsored class on shamanism seemed odd, I signed up for it.

The class was comprised of eight students, all new to shamanism. The teacher worked as a social worker during the day.

The first night, she taught the history of shamanism, which included an overview of spirit guides, power animals and shamanic journeying. She explained the different spirit realms, the purpose of power animals as guides and protectors, and the benefits of building relationships with spirit guides. I learned that shamanism is still practiced by indigenous people throughout the world today.

After an hour-and-a-half, her lesson seemed to be drawing to a close, so I was caught off-guard when she said, "Well, let's shamanic journey!" I had not even considered that someone other than a shaman could attempt this practice.

For six weeks, we journeyed to the spirit realm and shared our discoveries. The workshop turned out to be so much more than the history lesson I had expected!

The week after the workshop was completed, my family and I moved from Michigan to Florida. Since I didn't know any shamanic teachers in the area, I continued to shamanic journey on my own. Every few weeks, for reasons I didn't understand, I would hear a call to shamanic journey that was too strong to resist. I would wait until the house was empty, play my drumming CD and journey to the spirit realm.

After shamanic journeying for several years and relocating to West Palm Beach, I saw an advertisement for an upcoming event at a local metaphysical bookstore. A man named William, who claimed to channel an enlightened being, was offering a group reading.

Intrigued, I drove to the plaza where the metaphysical store was located. Melodious chimes greeted me as I walked through the entrance and saw a wide array of New Age books, jewelry, crystals and artwork. I proceeded to the back where rows of chairs had been arranged to face the raised platform on which William would be sitting while he channeled messages. I chose a chair in the front row and waited to see what would happen.

William walked onto the stage and sat down. He closed his eyes and, after a short while, he opened them and pointed to a woman. He told her she was trying to sell her house. She nodded in agreement. He gave her a time frame and instructions on how to best handle the offer. Another man was told that the software he was developing would be successful and not to give up—he was going to make a lot of money in addition to helping other people. Needless to say, the man diligently wrote down all the details.

After an hour, it seemed that most of the participants had been given a message for dealing with the realities of their lives. There were only a few people still waiting, and I started to worry that he had overlooked me.

I waited anxiously as William paused between messages and wondered who he would choose next. Suddenly he opened his eyes, pointed his finger at me, and shouted, "You are a healer!"

I honestly looked behind me, but when I turned back, he was still looking at me. Then he said, "One day you will be up here where I am, healing and teaching others."

The spirit he channeled told him that I had hidden from the role of being a healer because I had been persecuted for my talents in past lives. The channeled message continued for nearly 10 minutes—much longer than the other readings. I felt myself becoming embarrassed at the amount of time dedicated to describing healing abilities that I doubted I possessed. But the message made an impact on me, and somewhere in the back of my mind, the idea of being a healer churned.

A few months later, "Jessica," a friend who suffered from clinical depression, was having a mental breakdown. She'd had many such episodes in the previous years, and each one resulted in a minimum stay of a week at a psychiatric hospital while they reviewed her medications and sometimes performed electroshock treatments. It would then take her a week or two to recover at home.

I thought, "Why not shamanic journey to request a healing? After all, I am supposed to be a healer."

Since it was the first time I had requested a healing, I asked my power animal to show me the way. He led me to a spirit guide who accepted the healing request for Jessica.

Instantly the spirit guide and I were at the edge of Jessica's bed. The spirit guide symbolically opened up the top of her head and began to spin her brain. He called it a "spiritual lobotomy".

I asked if he could do anything for her pain. He sprinkled a white powder inside her head and said,

"Just a little something to take the edge off."

I thanked him for doing the healing, but still the vision did not seem real.

The next morning, I called Jessica and was shocked when she answered the phone. When I told her I was surprised, she said she was too! In fact, earlier that morning, she and her therapist had tried to analyze why she woke up feeling so good, but Jessica couldn't think of anything she had done that contributed to alleviating her depression.

Excited by the healing's success, I began performing healings for sick friends and family members who came to my attention. And it worked every time—even though most didn't know I had journeyed for them.

My life as a healer had begun, but I had not yet received the title of Shaman. However, it seemed fitting that my initiation as a shaman would be linked to my first healing.

Two years had passed since my first healing for Jessica when she sent me an email describing an amazing dream she'd had the night before. She said the dream was so vivid that it had to be real—an unusual statement from a woman who didn't practice any sort of spirituality or metaphysical activities.

In her message, she wrote that my spirit guide had come to her and said, "Today, we are celebrating Elizabeth becoming a Shaman!"

He asked her to join him and the other spirits as they celebrated my initiation. Jessica watched as the spirits danced around a fire and was mesmerized by the beauty and love of the ceremony. She saw them place a beautiful purple headdress on my head and proclaim that I was now a Shaman!

Jessica didn't know that earlier that day I had gone to a metaphysical bookstore and healing center to offer my shamanic healing services to the public for the first time—an improbable coincidence.

We all play a part in each other's lives, and no healing ever affects just one person. The very definition of a healing is two people recognizing their oneness.

As a modern shaman, I had no expectations or rituals to follow. I came with an open mind. I knew no limits and, therefore, never limited what I believed healing could achieve. If the spirits told me something, I believed them. It seemed simple, and it was.

Until this point, I had been performing healings

through shamanic journeying as an atheist, which I guess proves you don't have to believe in something for it to be true, but after a few years of healing others, I had begun to question where the power came from. This thought had persistently nagged me for several weeks when my mother called. While we discussed the healings I had been performing, she asked, "Where do you think God fits into all this?"

I replied that if God was part of the healings, He certainly was more than capable of showing Himself. As I said this, an energetic pressure began pushing down on the top of my head and flowing through my body. It became so intense that I couldn't lift my head. I literally was resting my head on the desk trying to talk. Finally I said, "Mom, I'm going to have to call you back," and ran to my room to shamanic journey.

Instead of the journey taking me to my spirit guide, I was led to a realm where Jesus stood to greet me. I was stunned. As a kid, I would often talk with Jesus, but it had been so long since I thought of Him or even believed He existed. Now He stood before me with welcoming arms. There was no judgment or condemnation for my lack of faith. I was overcome with joy and walked toward Him.

He said, "Welcome back. We have so much to do! Together, we can heal. You remember all the healings that I performed while on earth. Together, you and I can do so much more."

Although I was very happy that Jesus had returned to my life, I was skeptical of being able to heal on a full-time basis.

So I said, "Well, I can't pull gold coins out of fishes' mouths like you can. I have to work for a living." (Yes, I know how bad it sounds talking to Jesus like that, but He understands.)

Instead of becoming angry, He smiled and said, "Hold out your hand." And I did. He placed two gold coins in my palm and said, "I will take care of you. Go and do what needs to be done."

Six months later, as the economy took a turn for the worse in 2007, my graphic design business was no longer sustaining me. For financial reasons, I accepted a position as an art director at a mattress company and was to start in a few weeks. Accepting this job meant walking away from a company that I had owned for over 15 years that had been very lucrative up until recently. In addition, I was taking care of my

16-year-old dog who was dying of congestive heart failure. Needless to say, I didn't feel blessed and was angry about my dog's imminent death.

Perhaps because I needed comforting, or for reasons I may never know, I was about to experience one of my life's greatest miracles.

The miracle occurred one morning while I was showering in our octagon-shaped walk-in shower. Its angled walls each held a half-moon window that offered a panoramic view of the sky and the clouds that floated by.

I was shampooing my hair when I looked out one of the shower windows and saw the face of God! It was perfect! It was as if an artist had chiseled God's face out of a solid block of cloud. Every detail was there—hair, eyebrows, eyes, nose, mouth, and even a mustache and beard. I stood there stunned. One part of me was in awe of the miracle, and another part of me thought how perfectly natural it felt to see "God". I stood there staring until the shampoo began to run down my face. I turned to rinse the shampoo, but when I looked back, only a few remnants of God's beard and hair remained. It was as if a giant hand had wiped the face away.

Immediately doubt began to set in. My mind began to rationalize that while it might be a billion-to-one chance of God's face appearing in perfect detail, it could have been a natural phenomenon. Yet the other part of my mind was saying, "It would have to be a completely calm day to have that kind of detail appear, yet the face was 'blown away' in a few seconds...Why shouldn't God appear?...He's capable of anything!"

As my mind went back and forth from awe to doubt, I began massaging conditioner through my hair, looking out one of the other shower windows. I was shocked to see God's face staring at me for a second time! It looked exactly like the first one. I glanced back to the other window and could still see the remnants of the first face there. Even my logical mind couldn't deny this one. I turned back to gaze at God's face, realizing that He was giving me a sign that I could not dispute. Seeing His face erased any doubt I had of His existence and proved to me that He is more than capable of showing Himself.

Finally I turned away to rinse the conditioner out of my hair. When I looked back, the face had been swept away. And just like the first one, only a few wispy remnants remained as evidence of the miracle.

A few weeks later, my dog passed peacefully at home, and the following week, I started my new job. Life seemed normal, but after a few months, it became apparent that I was neither happy working for someone else nor fulfilling my life's purpose. I felt that the Spirit was calling me to leave Florida and that my life's path lay somewhere else. The only problem was, I had no idea where that other place was.

My husband and I both left our jobs in July 2008 and used our tax refund to pay for a two-week road trip. We planned to visit cities in North Carolina, Georgia, and Virginia, as well as family in Michigan.

The road trip would offer lots of time to read in the car, so I began searching for books to bring along. However, nothing in the bookstores stood out, and I had read everything in the house except for one book, *A Course in Miracles* (ACIM). My father had given me the book several years earlier, but I had only read the first page to where it said, "All miracles mean life, and God is the Giver of life." When I saw the word "God," I stopped reading and put the book back on the shelf where it had been sitting ever since collecting dust.

However, my viewpoint on God had changed since then. And although I believed ACIM was a textbook for a theology college course, I was willing to read it to see how it claimed miracles occurred and compare its thought process to shamanism.

It turned out that ACIM was not a college textbook. Instead, I learned the writings were channeled and dictated by Helen Schucman and put into words by William Thetford, both professors at Columbia University's College of Physicians and Surgeons in New York City. The channeling was a strange occurrence to have happened to an atheist.

The book was written in Shakespearean verse and difficult to comprehend, but riding in the car provided the perfect situation for absorbing the complex reading material. I would read a few paragraphs or a page at a time, and then aimlessly gaze at the passing landscape while my brain processed the teachings. Once the message was digested, I would resume reading again. At times, I would be completely immersed in the message and hear its "voice" talking to me.

I was surprised that I could not find anything in ACIM that contradicted shamanism. In fact, its teachings added valuable insight into how shamanic healing occurs. For example, ACIM teaches that there are spiritual teachers, such as Jesus and others, who provide guidance to those of us who are still in human form. In shamanism, these teachers would be called spirit guides.

ACIM speaks of miracles altering the past to heal the present and thereby changing the future. I had already seen how shamanic healing could cut karmic ties to people's pasts to heal their present lives.

ACIM teaches that through forgiveness we remove the blockages from our minds, which keep us from knowing our spiritual selves and achieving wholeness. In shamanism, shamans perform soul retrievals to search and retrieve lost soul parts to help restore the soul to wholeness. Whether you call it blockages or lost soul parts, both have the same goal of wholeness.

After the road trip, my husband and I came home discouraged. We hadn't liked any of the cities we visited, didn't have jobs, and had no idea where we wanted to live.

I tried to shamanic journey for answers, but I didn't receive any, so I asked for guidance from several outstanding psychics that I personally knew. Each one of their readings had a common message: "Move to North Carolina."

We had already visited Charlotte, North Carolina, on our earlier road trip, but we hadn't felt it was right for us. Nonetheless, we decided to give the state another chance. My husband and I got out a map, performed Internet searches, and read books that helped determine the Raleigh metro area would be a good choice.

We set out on another road trip and spent five days sightseeing cities and towns filled with rolling hills, lush trees and friendly people. As we drove past a park with a carousel filled with kids, I commented to my husband that Raleigh seemed like the town Mayberry from The Andy Griffith Show. I continued to gaze at the picturesque playground of people having picnics and cruising in paddle boats when I noticed a bronze statue of Andy Griffith and Opie holding a fishing rod. That was the clincher. We agreed it would be a good place to raise our two children. We found a house in a small town outside of Raleigh and headed back to Cape Coral, Florida, to pack.

The night before we moved, my husband saw a shooting star and mentioned to me that he hadn't seen one in years. The next evening, we headed off to Jacksonville, Florida, where we would spend the night before continuing to North Carolina. As we pulled into the hotel parking lot, a shooting star fell over the hotel—it felt like we were following guiding stars!

A few weeks after the move while driving home from an evening ACIM gathering, I started to think how crazy it had been to move to a different state based on psychic readings. I had lost my mind! I remembered how the shooting stars had shown themselves at the beginning of our move, but neither my husband nor I had seen one since we settled in North Carolina.

Panic started to set in, so I asked the Spirit for a sign, "Please show me a shooting star if this is where I am supposed to be right now."

Immediately a shooting star appeared! But it fell along the edge of a grain silo, and I wondered if maybe it had been a headlight reflection (there is no limit to my mind's ability to cast doubt). I asked the Spirit to please send me a second shooting star, since I was unsure about the first one. As soon as I finished the request, a shooting star fell in the middle of the night sky! Finally there was no doubt in my mind that this was where I was supposed to be. And as I drove down the road, the streetlights flickered off, one by one.

Because I have seen so many miracles, I know they occur. But to really understand how and why miracles happen, you either need to experience them yourself or vicariously learn through others.

This book offers true-life stories of miracles. Miracles can be daily events. All you have to do is ask.

Blessed journeys!
Elizabeth M. Herrera

# Introduction

I have experienced many miracles that have opened my eyes to the oneness of everything—even a grain of sand contains the entire universe within its being.

This book contains a collection of stories that illustrates miracles do occur. A miracle is known by its effect, although its power source is unseen. Like gravity, we see an apple fall from the tree, and so, we know it exists. But how a miracle transpires from the initial request to the final transformation is often a mystery to people.

It's said that a picture is worth a thousand words, so I have tried to paint a picture of miracles. The true-life stories in this book help to demonstrate that miracles do happen and everyone is capable of receiving and giving them. There is no special power. All true power comes from our loving Creator and is equally shared.

Miracles occur when two
people realize that there is no
separation between them.

In that moment, love flows freely and
their true reality becomes known.

Their perfectness is acknowledged
and they are released from the
illusion of fear, pain and illness.

# Different Perspectives

"As a man thinketh, so does he perceive. Therefore, seek not to change the world, but choose to change your mind about the world."

— *A Course in Miracles*

Although I had been shamanic journeying for several years, I had only been performing healings for a couple of months when my husband, Jon, became ill.

He was rushed to an emergency room with severe pain in his lower abdomen and was later admitted to the hospital. But after four days, an MRI scan and a team of doctors working on him, he was sent home with no diagnosis.

However, he kept having painful attacks, and each time he was rushed back to the emergency room. The medical bills were stacking up fast, and the doctors didn't have an answer. Finally a nurse quietly told us in the emergency room that he had the symptoms of Crohn's disease and to see a specialist.

The nurse was right and my husband was diagnosed with Crohn's, which is an incurable, chronic illness that causes extreme pain in the lower intestinal track.

After a few months of debilitating pain and excessive weight loss, I asked my husband if I could perform a healing for him. I had hesitated to ask him because I was concerned that if the healing didn't seem to work, it would confirm Jon's view that this "spiritual stuff" wasn't real, but to my surprise, he agreed to participate in the healing. However, I wasn't sure if he was just humoring me or willing to try anything at that point.

We laid down on our bed while I shamanic journeyed. A spirit guide appeared as a Native American medicine man. He was accompanied by a young man who served as his apprentice. The spirit guide sucked the sickness from my husband's intestines and spit it into a fire that burned in a stone bowl. He repeated this several times.

After the spirit guide finished the healing, he gave me the results—my husband would be well in two weeks! But he pointed to a small, pink area in my husband's intestines and said Jon would always carry a part of the disease with him.

My husband was better within the given time frame and began to look for work.

Several months later, I went for my annual check up. Since my husband and I shared the same family doctor, he asked how Jon was doing.

When I told him my husband was fine and had gone back to work, the doctor immediately said, "That's not possible! He has only had this disease for six months. People with Crohn's suffer for the first two years and off-and-on for the rest of their lives! I have two other patients that have had Crohn's for several years, and they are miserable and in constant pain."

I shrugged my shoulders and said, "Well, he's fine."

The doctor insisted that he must have been mis-diagnosed and asked me to have him make an appointment and bring the x-rays.

My husband made an appointment, showed the doctor the x-rays, and they talked about his current medications and condition. The doctor agreed that

Crohn's seemed to be the correct diagnosis, but he was amazed that Jon was fine.

A year later, after we moved to southwest Florida, my husband's new doctor also questioned the Crohn's diagnosis. The doctor ordered a DNA marker test that indicates if someone is likely to have had Crohn's. It came back positive. He ordered a radiograph with dye, which showed that the area between the colon and large intestine was enlarged— another indication of Crohn's. The doctor believed that Jon did indeed have Crohn's, although he was now symptom free.

It has been five years since the healing, and my husband continues to do well. I am thankful that my husband has been able to lead a normal life and be an active husband and father.

My husband has no recollection of this healing. The mind is a funny thing and will only remember what it wants to remember. I had hoped that his miraculous healing would allow him to believe in miracles, but instead he believed in the wonders of modern medicine...even though the doctors hadn't believed it was possible for him to be healed. However, everyone has to travel along his or her own path. I honor his beliefs and appreciate his understanding as I honor mine.

### *Message from the Spirit*

*We all have our own road to follow. We do not want to be led or pushed. Rather, we want to find the truth at our own pace. He comes with an open mind that has not yet been ready to accept the things you say. So be it. Each lifetime is filled with the lessons we need to learn. Nothing more, nothing less.*

# The Wisest of Wise

"In the depth of winter, I finally learned that there was within me an invincible summer."
— Albert Camus

I met "Linda" in late December. My husband and I were having a house built in southwest Florida, and she was the builder's color consultant.

Linda patiently worked with me for hours selecting the tiles, paint, roofing, lighting, and other miscellaneous items that needed to be ordered for the new house. Afterward, we drove around looking at tiled roofs, so I could have a better idea of how the showroom samples would look after they were installed. We had fun that afternoon and started to build a friendship.

Around this time, I began to have a recurring dream of an old woman who lived at the base of a mountain. She would stand in her kitchen and ask me to come to her. I could see the glass jars sitting on the window ledge in the kitchen, the staircase leading to the second floor, the goats that roamed behind the old farmhouse, and a stone path that led to the dirt driveway below.

The dream would repeat itself, and each time the old woman would ask me to come to her—claiming she had much to teach me. One night the dream differed, and I saw her go into town to meet with a lawyer and deed her property to me.

After a few months, the continual dream began to bother me and I felt compelled to go to her, but I had no idea where she lived. The only thing I knew for certain was I was running out of time—she would be dead in July and it was already the end of May.

Finally I couldn't take it anymore and told my husband I was going on a road trip, but I had no idea where I was going or when I would be back. He took it pretty well.

The night before I planned to leave, I asked the Spirit to give me an answer on where to go, but in the morning, I felt let down because I had not received an answer.

After showering, I was sitting on the bed wondering what to pack and how to proceed when the phone rang. It was Linda calling to say hello and see what I was doing.

"I'm going on a road trip," I said.

"Oh, where to?" Linda asked.

"I don't know," I replied.

Linda paused and then asked, "Do you want to talk about it?"

Then I paused. How do you tell a new friend about a vivid dream that speaks so powerfully that you feel forced to follow it? She knew nothing about the healings I had been performing.

Nonetheless, I decided to take a risk and tell her about the dream. I described the old woman who kept calling to me, the farmhouse that was nestled on a mountain, the goats and stone path, and even the inheritance that had been set up with a lawyer, then I waited for her response.

Linda slowly said, "You just described my grandmother to a tee. She lived on a hundred-acre farm in Missouri at the base of the mountains. She had goats, loved to can, and often set jars in the kitchen window. My father built that stone path. There is even an old Indian trail and camp at the back of her farm."

"But I have to get to her before she dies in July!" I blurted out. Then my heart stood still as I realized how insensitive my words had been, and I hoped Linda wouldn't be too upset at the bad news.

"Elizabeth, my grandmother died last July. We are having a memorial service for her this July," she calmly replied.

My first thought was "I am too late!" And then I realized that the old woman had never been talking to me. She was Linda's grandmother and had been trying to talk to her through me.

Linda continued, "You were right about everything except the inheritance. She didn't have much and the farm went to her kids. But since you have such a strong connection to her, why don't you join me when I go back to the farm for her memorial service? You can see the farm for yourself."

I was very tempted to go with her, but I felt that I would be out of place at the family event and declined. (I have always regretted not going.)

In July, Linda called when she returned home from the memorial service.

She said, "You are not going to believe this, but there was a small inheritance! My grandmother left us grandkids burial plots and a little money in a trust to help maintain the family cemetery. It's not much, but she had prearranged it and wanted to surprise us with it at the memorial service. You were right about everything!"

We thought that Linda's grandmother had simply wanted to reach out to her through me, but the real reason Linda's grandmother had contacted me was revealed the following month.

In the meantime, my close friend "Regina" was diagnosed with breast cancer and I had performed a shamanic healing for her. During the healing, the spirit guides revealed that Regina's cancer had spread to her lymph nodes, but they were willing to "push the cancer back" into the lumps within her breasts to give her time to surgically remove the cancer. However, they cautioned that she needed to move quickly.

When I mentioned Regina's healing to Linda, she was curious and asked questions about how shamanic healing worked. She also revealed that she and others in her family were intuitive—although it had been suppressed due to religious convictions.

In August, I was overjoyed to receive the good news that Regina's surgery had been successful and the cancer had not spread.

However, the next day Linda called to tell me she had breast cancer. I felt like throwing up—too many women I cared about were dealing with breast cancer.

I asked her why she thought she had breast cancer. She answered that she had found lumps in her breast and under her arms and that cancer ran in her family. Her mother and two aunts had died from it, but she was waiting for her health insurance to start in a few weeks before going to the doctor. I told her I would request a healing for her.

Later that night, I decided to shamanic journey for Linda. I visited my spirit guide who usually performed the healings, but this time he pushed me away. I refused to leave, saying, "I need a healing."

He answered, "You need more than a healing. You need a miracle!"

A young Native American man appeared on a horse, and my spirit guide asked me to get on the other horse and follow him. Together, we rode along a mountain path. The scenery was beautiful, and, in the distance, I admired the snow-covered mountains and lush valley below.

The path led to a valley where a council of Native American chiefs sat in a circle around a fire. Each chief was from a different tribe and represented the wisest of wise.

I was invited to sit with them and smoke a pipe, which went around the circle several times before the leader asked me why I was there. I answered that I was requesting a healing for a friend. The pipe was passed again. Finally the leader spoke, asking why they should grant the request and what had my friend done to deserve it. Truthfully I didn't have an answer. I responded that I wanted the healing just because I asked. There was a lesson here—none of us has truly done anything worthwhile. It's our true essence, our spirit, that is deserving, just as it is. The leader considered my answer and agreed to do the healing.

He took a crystal, which he said represented ice, and like water that changes to ice when frozen, he would transform the cancer into a harmless substance of lymph fluid. He passed the crystal over her breast and under her arm where the lumps were.

He continued with his message and reminded

me of how I had escaped winter by moving from Michigan to Florida, but that everything has its place. Winter can cause some things to die, others to hibernate, but most endure the hardship. And in the spring, the new branches grow, the babies are born, and a new cycle begins. I must learn that everything is good, even those things I considered undesirable. Everything offers a lesson. Everything transforms. One day our body will die, but our spirit will live on.

I called Linda the next day to let her know I had journeyed to request a healing for her, but she responded that she already knew. I asked how, since I hadn't told her when I would journey. She said she had felt a presence come into her house. After making sure that there wasn't an intruder, she accepted that I must be journeying for her and relaxed, letting the spirits work on her. She said she felt their touch and presence. She even wrote down the time, so I would believe her. The confirmation gave her and me great comfort.

She went in for an MRI scan three weeks later. The lumps appeared to be solid and a biopsy was ordered. However, Linda kept her faith that everything would be all right. One week later on the day of the biopsy, another MRI scan was performed, but the lumps had changed. The doctor said they now appeared to be liquid-filled instead of solid and that the biopsy was now optional. Since everyone was there, Linda decided to go ahead with the biopsy. The results? Lymph fluid!

It has been four years since I performed the healing for Linda, and she continues to do well with no sign of cancer.

Unfortunately her sister was diagnosed with breast cancer a few years later. Expecting another miracle, Linda requested a healing for her sister.

Her sister's healing request went well, and the spirit guides offered her a complete healing. However, several days later when I was performing a healing for another person, Linda's sister appeared in a vision, and I looked to see if the cancer was gone, but I saw that the lump was still there. I asked the spirits why the cancer wasn't gone and was shown a silver string of light arched between the cancerous lump and her head. I understood the message to mean: "Her mind has not accepted the healing."

What does it cost to accept a miracle? The whole world! The body is a symbol of what you think you are, yet the spiritual mind can alter the body. When this happens, a person has to accept that this world is not as it seems—and that can be a frightening concept for most people.

The Divine source is willing to help us, but a healing is never forced on anyone.

Thankfully her sister's surgery and chemotherapy treatments were successful.

### *Message from the Spirit*

*What ascends upon us is not the problem but the symptom. All illness stems from the mind and all thoughts of illness can be removed from the mind.*

# Spirits of the Past, Present and Future

"THE MIRACLE EXTENDS WITHOUT YOUR HELP, BUT YOU
ARE NEEDED THAT IT CAN BEGIN. ACCEPT THE MIRACLE OF
HEALING, AND IT WILL GO FORTH BECAUSE OF WHAT IT IS. IT IS
ITS NATURE TO EXTEND ITSELF THE INSTANT IT IS BORN."

— A COURSE IN MIRACLES

The first time that I taught a shamanic journeying
class, an amazing miracle occurred.

The class was held at a metaphysical bookstore in
Fort Myers, Florida. Initially six students signed up
for the class, but as each week passed, fewer and fewer
students attended. However, there was one woman
who was eager to be there. "Irene" had shamanic
journeyed for years, but she had hit a blockage that she

couldn't seem to overcome and hoped the class would help her.

Every week Irene showed up ready to learn, and she made remarkable progress in her shamanic journeying skills, eventually moving past the blockage.

By the time the final class came around, Irene was ready to perform her first healing. Since she was the only student who showed up that evening, we agreed she would perform a healing for me and I would perform one for her.

My healing request was to know whether I should stay in the graphic design field, which had been my career for over 20 years, and Irene, who was contemplating leaving her husband, wanted to know if it was in her best interest to do so. She had a small child and very much wanted to keep her family intact, but her husband was emotionally distant and noncommunicative, and she was tired of working on the relationship.

After we had finished shamanic journeying, Irene offered her healing results first. In her journey, she had seen words being spray painted on a wall, but had been unable to read the message. Symbolically it seemed clear to me: The writing was on the wall. It was time to move on.

During the healing for Irene, I had asked the spirits to show me what Irene and her husband's life was like together, and I saw them sitting in the living room—each in their own seat. There didn't appear to be anything out of the ordinary, so I requested to see how she would fare without her husband, and three spirits came and escorted him away. I then saw her sitting there alone, but not much else changed. It seemed for her whether he was there or not had little impact.

The vision continued and I saw Irene and her husband getting married, which was odd since they were obviously already married. Her husband was waiting for her at the altar—although he looked like the beast from Beauty and the Beast. Then I was shown the two of them having romantic interludes with bubble baths and champagne, and him offering her pearls.

When the healing was over, I described the vision to Irene, but it didn't make sense to either of us at the time. However, she called me several days later very excited to share what had happened since the healing.

Irene said that after the class, she went home to what seemed like an ordinary evening. She had taken care of a few things and gone to bed without saying much to her husband or discussing the healing.

During the night, Irene was awakened by her husband, who was sobbing. When she turned to him, he began hugging her and repeatedly telling her how much he loved her. He then asked her to renew their marriage vows! He explained that three spirits had visited him. The spirits of the past, present and future had shown him his entire life and spoken of the importance of their marriage for his spiritual growth.

The visiting spirits had an immense impact on her husband, who had a complete transformation, which led to a renewal of their love and passion for each other. As Irene put it, "The sex was better than when we first met!" And I was thinking, "If only I could package this!"

Both Irene and I were surprised at how the healing had affected her husband. The healing demonstrated that a miracle can extend itself in ways that we can't even begin to imagine.

## *Message from the Spirit*

*The purpose of the healing was not to restore their marriage, but to restore their spiritual path. The restoration of the marriage was a fringe benefit. Although many are shown the way to enhance their spiritual path, most choose not to follow. Time itself was made by you to avoid returning to your true selves, and most, when given a choice, will turn away from what is so clearly seen and simple to follow.*

*A healing was provided, divine intervention was given, and the path was shown. The decision to follow, or not, was entirely theirs.*

# Talking with Hurricanes

"FORGET NOT THAT THE EARTH DELIGHTS TO FEEL YOUR BARE
FEET AND THE WINDS LONG TO PLAY WITH YOUR HAIR."
— KAHLIL GIBRAN

In 2004, the first major hurricane since Hurricane
Andrew was headed toward South Florida. My family
and I had moved to Florida two years earlier from
Michigan and were inexperienced in how to deal
with Hurricane Frances headed our way.

We asked our friends and neighbors for advice
on how to prepare for the possible storm, and
relied on the meteorologists' projections for where
and when the hurricane would hit. Day after day,
computer-generated weather reports flashed across
the television screen offering a multitude of possible
paths the hurricane might follow, and, although the

hurricane had gotten closer to us, it was traveling much slower than originally predicted. I was beginning to doubt the science community's capacity to accurately forecast the path of a hurricane.

We were prepared to stay. My husband had already put up the shutters, which took a full day and was no small feat in the blazing hot sun. The outdoor furniture had been brought inside, and we were stocked up on food, water, flashlights, batteries, and gas for the cars.

However, if we were going to evacuate, we would have to leave at least two days before the hurricane was scheduled to hit, or we would be stuck on I-95 in bumper-to-bumper traffic.

Still, we hesitated to leave. We didn't want to travel to another state only to discover that Hurricane Frances had weakened into a Category 1 hurricane or had headed up the coast and missed Florida completely.

After many frustrating days of not knowing whether to stay or go, I decided to shamanic journey for an answer.

I lay down to journey and was immediately connected to Hurricane Frances, which appeared in the form of a giant woman made of water (sort of like the Michelin Man). She came storming toward me, and each footstep thundered and shook the ground. When she got to the edge of the shore, she slammed her fist down. A great thud vibrated the land for miles. She then slammed down her other fist with the same intensity. This vision repeated itself two more times.

When I got up, I knew not only would Hurricane Frances hit Florida, but also that a second hurricane would follow in its path. I told my husband to pack— we were leaving!

As we drove on the highway into Georgia, we noticed that most of the license plates were Floridian. It was a mass exodus—like rats fleeing a sinking ship!

When we arrived at the hotel in Chattanooga, Tennessee, the hotel clerk said we were lucky we arrived early. An Internet travel site had overbooked their rooms, and those arriving later would have to be turned away.

On September 4, 2004, Hurricane Frances hit as a Category 2 hurricane. She was a huge, slow-moving storm that caused massive property damage and power outages throughout all of South Florida, and the upper parts of the state as she made her way inland, finally exiting near Tampa into the Gulf of Mexico.

We stayed four days in Chattanooga, but when it became clear that Florida was going to take awhile to recover, we decided to drive to Michigan and visit our families. During the impromptu vacation, we enjoyed celebrating our daughter's sixth birthday with her cousins, aunts, uncles, and grandparents.

I was grateful we'd left. Not only did we avoid sitting in a dark house listening to our roof tiles fly off, we also didn't have to endure Florida's hot summer with no electricity or air conditioning, limited access to food and gas, and imposed curfews to reduce looting.

A week after we returned home, we had to evacuate again, because Hurricane Jeanne was headed our way. She hit within one mile of Hurricane Frances—two hurricanes within three weeks!

A few years later, I used the gift of talking to storms with Hurricane Noel, which was predicted to hit southwest Florida, where we now lived. Again, I wondered whether we should evacuate.

Hurricane Noel was currently a tropical storm passing over Cuba, causing many people to die in mudslides and floods, but he was slated to become a major hurricane when he passed over the warm waters of the Gulf of Mexico.

I shamanic journeyed and waited for Hurricane Noel to connect with me. When he finally appeared, he seemed pleasant, so I introduced myself and said, "I want to know if you are headed my way. I don't want to influence you, I just need to know whether or not my family should leave."

Hurricane Noel asked, "Why would you leave?"

I replied, "Because you can hurt people. We are fragile and easily broken. Many people have already died where you are now."

He seemed sad as he spoke, "I am lonely and like being around people. I don't want to hurt anyone."

And then our connection went black.

The next morning, I checked The Weather Channel's website and was shocked to see that Hurricane Noel's path, which had been weaving over the Caribbean islands, had taken an abrupt right turn away from Cuba during the night. He remained a tropical storm until he hit the open and unpopulated waters of the Atlantic Ocean where he let his glorious powers bloom into a hurricane.

It appeared that the conversation between Hurricane Noel and me had impacted him (and perhaps he talked with others as well), and he decided to take a route that wouldn't harm additional people. I think this quote from Deepak Chopra explains it well: "The universe is alive and conscious, and it responds to our intent when we have our intimate relationship with the universe and see it not as separate but as our extended body."

From a shamanic perspective, everything has a spirit. The earth, rivers, moon, stars, trees, and weather elements each has a spirit. We need to look at our balance with nature, which is alive and waiting to connect with us. Our urban lifestyles have cut us off from feeling the earth beneath our feet, dancing in the rain, and telling a storm cloud how much we appreciate its presence. The next time it rains, stand outside, and let the rain touch you. It's alive!

## *Message from the Spirit*

*A voice is heard calling from the willow, but you turn your head. A caress comes from the wind, yet you tighten your coat. The sun infuses you with knowledge, instead you feel scorched. Surrender to the forces, become one, and let them lead you to your greatness.*

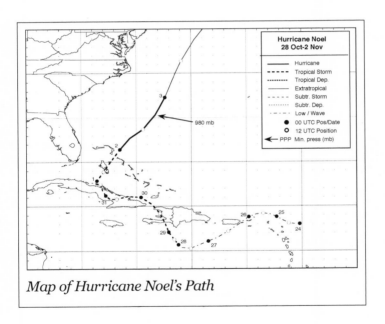

*Map of Hurricane Noel's Path*

# Deadly Canal

"I WANT TO DIE IN MY SLEEP LIKE MY GRANDFATHER...NOT SCREAMING AND YELLING LIKE THE PASSENGERS IN HIS CAR."
— WILL SHRINER, COMEDIAN

Cape Coral, Florida, is a unique city, built on a peninsula that extends into the Gulf of Mexico near Fort Myers. It has hundreds of gulf-access canals dug by enterprising businessmen who thought they would create the world's largest trailer park, but they went bankrupt, and the narrow lots were combined to make double and triple lots on which houses could be built.

Cape Coral is the second largest city in Florida, in terms of geographical area, and still has many empty lots on which to build. It's an odd sight seeing beautiful Mediterranean-styled houses next to weed-covered lots, mile after mile. It was here that my sister and I lived in houses on salt-water canals, a few blocks from each other.

One night, three young men driving home from a club missed a doglegged curve and drove their car through an empty lot, plunging into a canal. Although the canal was 150 feet wide, their car had sailed almost to the other side.

My sister woke up to a strange sound. Thinking that one of her animals was in pain, she rushed into the living room to check on them, but realized that the sound was coming from outside. She opened the sliding glass door and stood by the pool where she heard a neighbor yelling across the dark waters of the canal, "Swim to the sound of my voice!" From the canal, my sister heard a man emit a garbled, high-pitched scream for help—then it was quiet.

As the neighbors gathered near the seawall, my sister learned that one of them had seen a car plunge into the canal, but there was no sign of the men, car, or even a headlight beam. All three men had drowned.

The red-and-blue lights of the police cars flashed as the policemen searched in vain during the night, trying to locate the missing bodies. A police helicopter flew overhead shining a spotlight over the scene while scuba divers probed the murky waters. Meanwhile, local TV news crews were busy reporting and interviewing witnesses. It turned out the young men were only a block from their house.

The next afternoon, my sister observed the recovery of the car and a body being pulled out of the water by scuba divers.

That evening, a friend called me to ask how my sister was doing after witnessing this traumatic event, but as I began answering her, my right arm suddenly went limp. It felt as if a presence had entered through the top of my shoulder and taken control of my arm. I became alarmed because nothing like that had ever happened to me before.

I immediately got off the phone and shouted at the presence, "No! You're not coming into me!" The presence seemed to leave, and within moments, I regained the use of my arm.

A few days later while slowly driving on a quiet street to my sister's house, I viewed the sparkling blue waters of the canals thinking about the young men who died in the accident. As I neared the canal where they had drowned, my arm went limp again. This time I was calm, because it became obvious that the presence was one of the young men trying to contact me. I began to talk to him, speaking gently as I delivered the tragic news, "I don't know if you know this or not, but you died in a car accident. Remember coming home from the club? Well, your car went into a canal and all of you drowned."

I waited for his response. I knew he was listening and remembering what had happened.

"I know this seems traumatic, but you are going to be all right. However, you do need to move on."

He stated that he was afraid and did not know where to go.

"Let me show you," I said. "Follow me."

I let my mind float up to the clouds, which parted to reveal two of his relatives standing at the edge waiting for him.

"Do you see them?" I asked.

"I do!" he responded.

"Go to them. It will be all right." I said encouragingly.

He went to greet his loved ones, and then they faded from view.

The next time I spoke of the young men's accident, my arm was perfectly fine.

### *Message from the Spirit*

*A soul needed help. He reached out to a person who could hear his plea. He went from a scared soul to one joined with his loved ones. All healing is done within the spirit, whether a person has a body or not, is not important.*

# Wheelchair Bound

One day, my friend "Sara" mentioned she was planning to go to dinner with her old friend "Sam," who needed cheering up.

Sam was suffering from Crohn's disease, which my husband also had suffered from, so I sympathized with his condition. Besides experiencing unbearable pain, the stress on Sam's body had led to diabetes and allowed an unknown, but preexisting, condition of hepatitis to surface.

Because of pain and fatigue, Sam was wheelchair bound, unable to work and penniless. And to throw grease on the fire, his wife couldn't deal with it and had left him. If he were a country singer, he would have had a hit song!

That evening, I was shamanic journeying to ask for financial guidance, because the healing requests were not paying the bills. A spirit guide appeared who had long, white hair and wore a robe. My request for financial guidance seemed of no importance to him. Instead he said, "Don't TRY to be a healer...you are a healer!" Then he asked if I knew anyone who needed healing.

The only person who came to my mind was Sara's friend Sam.

The spirit guide performed Sam's healing, then stated that he would be healed within one month.

The next day, I called Sara, but she didn't answer her phone, so I left a message with the details of Sam's healing and hoped she would get it before their dinner that evening.

She did get the message and called me immediately after dinner to let me know how receptive Sam had been to the good news. It turned out Sam had grown up in the Florida Everglades, and most of his boyhood friends that lived there were Native American. He was familiar with shamanic healing and had faith in its power.

Sara said, "Sam is going to write the date on his calendar so we can go to dinner to celebrate his healing."

I was surprised and happy to learn of Sam's willingness to accept the healing, but I had grown so accustomed to relinquishing healing outcomes to the Spirit that I had forgotten about it until Sara called me a month-and-a-half later.

"Sam is healed!" she said.

"Who?"

"You know, my friend who was in the wheelchair."

Then I remembered. "How's he doing?" I asked.

"He's feeling so good that he started hunting and fishing again. And you know how he hasn't been able to work. Well, a friend asked to use his contractor's license and is giving him 10 percent of everything he makes. He got a check last week and would love to treat you to dinner to say thanks!"

The gift of a miracle, especially when it comes from someone you've never met, is a beautiful thing. It reminded me of the time when I was exploring a small island in the middle of the Caloosahatchee River, which flows into the Gulf of Mexico.

My husband would often navigate our pontoon to the island we nicknamed Chicken Bone Island because of all the fried chicken remains that were scattered about. We'd anchor the pontoon and wade to the sandy shore where the kids and dogs would run wild.

However, one sunny afternoon, I wanted to explore the uncharted center of the island that was populated with Saw Palmetto shrub. It was a struggle to push through the spiny brush while being careful to look for snakes.

As the path disappeared and the shrubbery became denser, I began to doubt the sanity of this adventure and was ready to turn around when I walked through a giant spider web. Frantically I started ripping the webbing from my head and neck, afraid that the spider that weaved it was crawling on me! As I paused to catch my breath, I noticed that a large beetle that had been entangled in the spider's web was now stuck to my arm. I screamed, grabbing the webbing, throwing it to the ground. The beetle bounced when it hit the sandy dirt, releasing it from the sticky snare. It seized the opportunity and quickly crawled away.

That beetle's situation had seemed hopeless, and

yet, out of nowhere, a crazy woman came trampling through the isolated dense brush, screaming, flailing her arms, and flinging him to freedom. For that beetle, it was a miracle.

And for Sam, a man who had sat helpless in a wheelchair, penniless, and in terrible pain, a miracle had come out of nowhere, just when he needed it most.

### *Message from the Spirit*

*A higher power does exist. The forces of day-to-day reality seem to take hold and become the truth for you, yet truth is not seen with the eyes or heard with the ears. It is felt as the peace in your heart and professes itself with health and well being.*

# Unwanted House Ghost

"LIFE IS PLEASANT. DEATH IS PEACEFUL. IT'S THE TRANSITION THAT'S TROUBLESOME."

— ISAAC ASIMOV

I remember once when my husband and I were considering the purchase and restoration of an historic house in St. Petersburg, Florida, that had most recently been used as a senior living home.

As we walked through the interior, a very uncomfortable feeling came over me, but I tried to stay analytical to estimate the restoration costs. Besides being in disrepair and gloomy, dark shadows seemed to dart across the hallways and through the rooms. After a hurried inspection, I couldn't take it anymore and left—quickly!

It's understandable why people are afraid of

ghosts or negative energy in their homes. It can be uncomfortable and sometimes scary, but a healing gave me a new insight into ghosts.

One day, I received a call from a woman asking me to perform a house depossession. For many years she had owned a rental house that was haunted by a ghost who appeared as a friendly, older woman. The tenants hadn't minded her presence and would often kindly refer to her.

Then a new tenant moved in and the ghost made him uncomfortable. The tenant tried to ignore the ghost, but she grew bolder. One night, the ghost entered his bedroom, walked up to his bed, and told him, "Scoot over." That was too much for him! The man slept on the couch that night and in the morning told the landlord he was moving out.

The landlord wanted to know if I could perform the house depossession that day, because she didn't want to lose the tenant, and if I could do it remotely since she lived in Utah. I answered yes to both questions, and later that day, I met the "ghost of the house".

The ghost was an elderly woman who was waiting for me with her "ghost" bags packed. The ghost said she knew the tenant and landlord didn't want her in the house and was ready to move on.

The ghost recalled living there with her husband and raising their children, who were now grown and had children of their own. Her recollection of fond memories made me see her as a "person" instead of a ghost...a person without a body. But her plans were to move into another house! I told her that wasn't in anyone's best interest. In order to continue her soul's journey, it was important for her to move to the next realm. Without a body, she wasn't experiencing the life lessons that were necessary for her soul's growth.

After she left, I shamanic journeyed to the spirit realm to meet with my spirit guide to confirm that she was gone. When I arrived, the ghost was sitting next to my spirit guide waiting for me. (It seemed that she was always one step ahead of me.) Everyone agreed, including her, that she had crossed over into the next realm, and then the angels took her away.

My spirit guide then recommended that angels go to the house to remove the residual energy, so that the tenant wouldn't sense the ghost's presence any longer.

I watched the angels descend into the house and cleanse the negative energy. Afterward, they infused positive energy by symbolically dropping flower petals.

I knew it was a powerful healing when not only the landlord called to thank me, but the tenant did as well. The tenant said the most powerful aspect of the whole situation was the feeling he had when entering the house. He had expected the negative energy to permeate the house, but instead, he walked into positive energy that was so intense, he felt a natural high all day long.

The healing affected the landlord, the tenant (who ordered several more healings for himself and family members), and the ghost. It shows how we are connected—whether we have a body or not.

### *Message from the Spirit*

*The dreams of life die hard. Letting go of these dreams and the futile struggle in achieving them is a desire that must be released, a threshold to cross, with or without a body.*

# Karmic Ties

A mother called me for a healing for her son, "Jeremy," who had become very angry and introverted at age 12 for no apparent reason. Over a decade of psychotherapy and medical procedures had produced no improvements and made her son leery of having more treatments. He had no friends, was depressed, and had made several suicide attempts. But no one understood why he felt this way, including himself.

During the shamanic healing, I asked my power animal to take me to the appropriate realm, since no one knew exactly what was wrong with Jeremy. I was guided to one of his past lives where I saw him walking along the road as a boy carrying water. A band of rebels came around the bend in a truck and stopped to harass him. They started beating him, and then speared him with sticks until he was dead. It was a senseless death at the hands of cruel young men.

I was then shown Jeremy's current life's spirit and saw that his energetic body had not fully developed. It was only large enough for the boy that he had been in the previous lifetime, leaving most of his upper body exposed and vulnerable to negative energy.

To heal his karma, I went back to his previous life to alter the events that had transpired. When I came back to the scene, he was walking along the road. However, this time, instead of being beaten and stabbed to death, he was accidentally hit by a car. The driver rushed to hold him, crying as he apologized to the dying boy. The death was tragic, but not cruel, and left no hard feelings that carried over to his present life. The feelings of hatred and anger no longer existed, and the karmic tie to the past was severed.

In a second healing, spirit guides removed his useless energetic body and created a new one that fully covered him. They also established that two angels would stand guard over him for protection and strength to help him face a world that he had formerly been unable to navigate without pain.

Although I hadn't told his mother exactly when I would be performing the healing, she knew. She said Jeremy called her that evening for no reason other than to talk for the first time in his adult life, and they had a lengthy conversation. She said it was especially notable because of the effort it took to make the call, which she had received on her sister's house line. Today of all days, he just had to talk with her!

He continued to make rapid progress, and his mother requested monthly healings to ensure that his energetic body would remain strong. I hesitated to perform so many healings, but she assured me that if I knew how much money she had spent on medical treatments over the last decade, I would understand that it was a small price to pay for his continued well being.

A year later, Jeremy had steadily progressed to become a well-adjusted young man who had made friends and was performing well in college.

### *Message from the Spirit*

*Pain exists only in the mind. Whether an event is real or not doesn't matter, only that the mind believes it is. Suffering can be suspended by achieving new beliefs and perspectives. We see what we want to see, and feel what we want to feel. Never doubt that the life you lead is the life you want.*

# Gas Station Dreams

"THERE ARE ONLY TWO WAYS TO LIVE YOUR LIFE. ONE IS AS THOUGH NOTHING IS A MIRACLE. THE OTHER IS AS THOUGH EVERYTHING IS A MIRACLE."

— ALBERT EINSTEIN

One night in October, I had a dream that was so powerful there was no doubt in my mind that it had really happened.

In the dream, I floated into a scene of a man pumping gas. I knew he was a pastor who was having trouble making a difficult decision. My spirit descended into his car and "sat" in the passenger seat to wait for him to finish pumping gas. The pastor got in, started the car, and drove slowly through the parking lot. He paused before pulling into the street. At that moment he felt my presence, and although he couldn't see me, he knew I was there. I apologized for the intrusion. In his thoughts, he said, "That's okay. I was thinking about going for a drive."

I knew he had changed his plans of going directly home, and instead, he decided to go for a long drive to ponder his difficult decision. I left him alone with his thoughts as he drove away.

When I woke up, I remembered the dream vividly and couldn't forget it for weeks. I kept looking for this man in public—expecting to meet him. But after a couple of months had passed and I hadn't yet met the pastor, the dream was tucked into the back of my mind.

Then one night, I pulled up to my gym and noticed a Red Cross blood mobile in the parking lot. I decided I would give blood, although I had never voluntarily donated blood before.

I walked up to the table set up temporarily in the gym's lobby. The young woman standing there asked if I had any health problems, and I said no. She asked if I was in good health and feeling well. I answered that I was feeling a little light headed, but she didn't seem to hear me and began talking with someone else while she handed me a folder with a stack of forms that needed to be filled out.

After my name was called, I walked through the chilly night to the large RV that served as the blood mobile. A young woman greeted me and escorted me to a tiny room where she asked me questions, pricked my finger to take blood, and attached a finger monitor to check my blood pressure. At this point, there was a problem. It seemed my pulse rate and blood pressure were too high, which was very unusual since I normally have low blood pressure. She mentioned that I might be stressed about giving blood and thought answering additional questions on a computer in the room would give me time to calm down.

I finished the questions and was waiting for the woman to return when a man entered and explained he was the supervisor. I knew I wouldn't be giving blood as soon as he sat down, but decided to let the conversation play out.

With a smile, he asked me how I was feeling. I answered that I felt fine. He said perhaps I was coming down with something and just didn't know it yet—that sometimes an undetected infection can make the blood pressure spike as the body fights it.

I mentioned that I was feeling light headed, but felt that it was a reaction from an intense healing session I performed earlier in the day.

The supervisor was surprisingly knowledgeable about shamanic healing and pointed out that a healing session should have lowered my blood pressure. I agreed with him. He continued asking me questions about the healings that I performed, saying that it was wonderful work to offer healings and appreciated my efforts.

His spiritual demeanor captured my attention, and I asked him how he knew so much about healing. He answered that he was a pastor of a church in a distant city. Suddenly it dawned on me that he was the pastor from my dream! I began telling him, "Several months ago you had a tough decision to make."

He nodded his head in agreement, and said a few months earlier he had to decide whether to stay at his church or become the new pastor at a church of a different denomination. His mind told him to stay with his current congregation, but he felt God was guiding him to leave. After much soul searching, he had decided to go to the new church.

When I described seeing him in my dream at the gas station and the interaction that had occurred, he remembered asking God for a sign and stated that he often went on long drives to think.

I had been waiting to meet him and was blessed to do so. What a wonderful confirmation for the two of us.

I knew the elevated pulse rate was divine intervention, and after leaving the blood mobile, I went to work out at the gym. It felt great!

### *Message from the Spirit*

*We are all divine spirits, helping others on conscious and unconscious levels. The past, present and future exist simultaneously—all lives, all events have already occurred—leaving you with memories of illusions that you pluck from the recesses of your mind. You have reached enlightenment because you have never left it. So you have the ability to act as an angel, reaching out to others, offering miracles and love, now.*

# The Gift of Schizophrenia

"WHEN YOU HAVE LOOKED ON WHAT SEEMED TERRIFYING, AND SEEN IT CHANGE TO SIGHTS OF LOVELINESS AND PEACE; WHEN YOU HAVE LOOKED ON SCENES OF VIOLENCE AND DEATH, AND WATCHED THEM CHANGE TO QUIET VIEWS OF GARDENS UNDER OPEN SKIES, WITH CLEAR, LIFE-GIVING WATER RUNNING HAPPILY BESIDE THEM IN DANCING BROOKS THAT NEVER WASTE AWAY; WHO NEED PERSUADE YOU TO ACCEPT THE GIFT OF VISION?"

— *A Course in Miracles*

The medical community views schizophrenia as a condition that can be treated but not cured. Schizophrenics are considered to have a mental illness with symptoms such as hallucinations, paranoid or bizarre delusions, and dysfunction—which are subdued with antipsychotic medications.

However, I believe that schizophrenics are not suffering from an illness, but rather, are extremely receptive to contact from spirits, and when they cannot ward off imposing negative spirits who have no regard for the schizophrenics' well being, they become overwhelmed, catatonic, anxious, depressed, and even suicidal with thoughts and visions that seem to be their own, but in reality, are instilled into their minds by outside forces.

With proper shamanic healing and training, which has been done successfully in indigenous tribes under the guidance of shamans, schizophrenics could learn to prevent the intrusion of loud, negative spirits, and allow only the loving spirits' quiet voices to be heard. They have the gift to become great healers and shamans.

I was given the chance to prove this belief when "Andrew," a schizophrenic, middle-aged truck driver, contacted me for a healing. He said he was constantly assaulted by negative voices and wanted relief.

After I requested his healing from my spirit guide, I emailed him these results:

> *"In the spirit realm, with my spirit guide, we began to perform an extraction and aura cleansing*

*on your energetic body. There were many extractions and it took awhile to remove them. Afterward, your aura was cleansed and then the angels came in with loving energy and infused you with it. They then built up your energetic body to prevent unwanted spirits and people's thoughts from entering. Your crown chakra was too open and was reduced to a much smaller size to prevent unwanted spirits from entering. An intention was set that only the most holy of spirits would be able to enter."*

After receiving my message, Andrew indicated that he had known I had completed the healing. When I inquired how he knew, he sent me a lengthy description of what he had experienced while I performed his healing.

The following is a portion of Andrew's description of the healing as he wrote it with the exception of a few grammatical corrections.

*"Elizabeth...I had been snoozing... before that I had been wondering*

*when you would do the healing.*

*Today, I was gently awakened by a soft voice that said, 'They're here.'*

*I then began to be aware of your very light presence...my eyes were still closed. It was then that I said, "Hi!" (Author's note: This was significant, because when the healing began, I said "Hi" to Andrew's spirit and was surprised when he said "Hi" back. I replied, "Oh, you know I am here," but I didn't mention this in my message to him.)*

*I felt as though there were two presences in the room other than you and me. The little voice said, 'Don't open your eyes!'*

*I lay there for a few seconds and then I saw the outline of two spirits. One of a living person and one not. The one that was no longer living seemed very 'live' and holy. The other one appeared to be witnessing something. As I was lying in bed, I felt very little other than calm and comfortable. I closed my eyes again. The voice said, 'That was him.' Seemingly referring to the 'live' one.*

*I lay still. The voice said now they're getting rid of the spirits. I still felt calm and comfortable and yet wondered because I didn't feel much. Then the voice said, 'Now the angels are here.'*

*I kept my eyes closed and waited. A few minutes passed as I tried to sleep so as not to be a nuisance. The little voice said, 'You're not a nuisance.'*

*After a few minutes, the voice said, 'It's okay, they're gone.'*

*I felt a little like a computer that had just come to life and wondered, 'Is there nothing more?'*

*My apartment was dark...I keep the shades closed most of the time. It was near sunset and a little of the westerly sunlight was creeping through.*

*I started to make myself a cup
of coffee, then the voice said, 'She's
gone.'...meaning you."*

While I always give my clients a description of their healing, this was the first time a client had given me one! It showed how spiritually connected he was.

A few weeks later, Andrew complained that his mind was too quiet! I encouraged him to give it more time to adjust to the lack of noise in his mind. The loving spirits are soft spoken and do not impose themselves on anyone.

Ten months later, he wrote to me stating that the negative voices were bothering him less and less. He was now able to control the spirits' abilities to contact him and was doing well.

### *Message from the Spirit*

*Schizophrenia is a two-edged sword. It is both a curse and a gift until it becomes a finely tuned instrument. Then what could cut and kill becomes a mechanism for separating the wheat from the chaff—a gift for healing.*

# Stray Cat

"WE CANNOT EVEN IMAGINE THE COMPLEX FORCES BEHIND
EVERY EVENT THAT OCCURS IN OUR LIVES. THERE'S A
CONSPIRACY OF COINCIDENCES THAT WEAVES THE WEB OF
KARMA OR DESTINY AND CREATES AN INDIVIDUAL'S PERSONAL
LIFE—MINE, OR YOURS."
— DEEPAK CHOPRA, *THE SPONTANEOUS FULFILLMENT
OF DESIRE*

For a month, I had a premonition that a stray cat
would be coming into my life, and I wondered when
it would appear. While driving, I would look for him
possibly hidden in the roadside grass, and when
walking the dogs, I'd hope the cat would cross our
path.

On a cold, rainy evening when the kids and I were
unloading groceries, my son spotted an orange tiger

cat in the bushes by our front door. The wet skinny cat was easily coaxed out from his hiding place and began to play with my son and daughter.

Unlike my sister, who is a cat magnet, I have never had a stray cat appear. But I had accepted the invitation from the universe, and now for the first time, a cat was waiting near the front door, hoping for some food and possibly a new home.

On the second day, we discovered that he had a large abscess on his back—most likely caused by another cat's bite. I grew worried, because years earlier I had a cat with the same condition who became extremely ill, and thoughts of expensive veterinarian bills danced through my head.

I decided to perform a shamanic healing.

In the shamanic journey to the spirit realm, I watched as my spirit guide performed the healing. First, he lanced the cat's abscess and then applied pressure to the open sore, which forced the pus out. The angels came to infuse the cat with positive energy for swift healing.

Afterward, I asked my spirit guide how the healing would transpire in the physical realm. I found out a few hours later.

In the afternoon, my son asked me to take a look at the cat's abscess. He thought there was something stuck in it. I examined it and discovered that part of the cat's hair had become hardened from the fluids leaking from the infected sore. I gently tugged at the stiff hair. It came off, along with the surrounding skin. It seemed that I had "lanced" the wound. We applied antibiotic cream and hoped for the best.

The next morning, the abscess was gone! Sometime during the night, all the pus had seeped out, and now the cat was busy licking the area to keep it clean.

It could have become life threatening with expensive vet bills, but instead, within a day, the problem had been solved. It seemed fitting that the cat who suddenly appeared in our lives would have a need of healing services.

After a small battle with my husband, we officially adopted the cat—naming him Pumpkin because of his bright, orange coat and in the spirit of Halloween that was a few days away.

A year later, Pumpkin is doing very well and loves to be hugged. His favorite place to nap is on top of the entertainment cabinet next to the faux greenery. When he wakes up and yawns with his canines bared, he resembles a tiger waiting to pounce on unsuspecting prey below. He has gained three pounds and sometimes answers to the nickname Plumpkin.

### *Message from the Spirit*

*This was a lesson in learning to accept what you desire, and taking the lead in making it so. Courage is seen in small details, as well as large triumphs. Restoring our inner reserves is accomplished by giving to others. We help ourselves when we help others.*

# A Good Day to Die

My 84-year-old grandfather was a proud man. His
father was Apache and mother was Spanish, and they
had toiled for many years before buying a small farm
in Michigan. As a child, my grandfather knew the
harsh reality of migrant farming and the instability of
constant relocation. He often joked he was the oldest
kid in fifth grade, too big to fit in the desks and the
only student shaving.

In his later years, he suffered from stomach cancer,
which led to the reconstruction of his stomach. He
also had painful tumors that continually had to be
removed. However, the most recent growths were

cancerous and aggressive, and for the first time, he agreed to chemotherapy.

I decided to shamanic journey to request a healing for him. During the journey, I did not meet the usual spirit guide who answered my healing requests. Instead, a woman with a beautiful stark face and long raven hair appeared, wearing a flowing black cape and riding a black horse. She motioned for me to follow her.

I walked behind her through ancient catacombs. The dark stone tunnel was lit with torches and the walls were lined with skeletons. At the end of the tunnel, it opened up to a night sky and we journeyed through the stars until they faded from view.

The woman rode through the blackness that sifted around the horse's hooves like obsidian sand. When she stopped, we stood in what appeared to be complete and utter nothingness. She lifted her hand, motioning to the void around us, saying, "This is what your grandfather is afraid of. That there is nothing after he dies...no heaven...no afterlife...nothing."

My grandmother had told me that my grandfather would wake up in the middle of the night and sit in the kitchen, just to make sure he didn't die in his sleep. The spirit guide's message had explained why he was afraid to die, but it was surprising, because I would often see my grandfather reading the Bible and openly praying. I thought he held a firm conviction in the concept of heaven after dying.

A few months later, while my grandfather was briefly staying in a nursing home to build his strength, my grandmother received a call from a nurse letting her know that he was ready to go home. My grandmother was excited and rushed to the nursing home to tell my grandfather that she was looking forward to his return, but when she arrived in his room, my grandfather told her that he wanted to die. He had asked God to take him that day and God had agreed.

He gave my grandmother scrap pieces of paper with sentiments and instructions written on them, so she wouldn't forget (her memory was faulty from a stroke she had a few years earlier). He also told her to tell everyone that he loved them. But my grandmother felt she was seeing a healthy man before her, so she went home to await his return.

In the middle of the afternoon, a representative from the nursing home called to let her know that my grandfather had passed away.

A healing is not always a physical healing. To me, my grandfather had been healed. He had accepted his death with dignity. He had come to firmly believe that he would go meet God and not dissolve into nothingness as he had feared earlier. I am proud of how he faced death. It was such an Apache way to die.

Two years later, during a shamanic journey, the spirit of my grandfather appeared in the middle realm. It was the first time since his passing that I had "seen" him, and I happily greeted him.

He immediately began talking about my grandmother, saying how much he missed her and that he wouldn't go without her.

It was then that I realized that my grandfather's spirit hadn't crossed over yet.

He asked me to tell my grandmother that he loved her, but I said I didn't want to—it might upset her. Besides, she was always talking about how she could feel his presence anyway. But my grandfather insisted. He wanted her to hear the words, "I love you!"

I did not want to call my grandmother and tell her "I talk to dead people." But I had promised my grandfather I would, so I called.

After an awkward moment when she didn't recognize my name (she doesn't hear well), I shouted, "I had a vision of grandpa and he said to tell you he loves you."

She cried with joy, "I knew it! I knew he was here! I can feel him all the time. Thank you for telling me."

Telling my grandmother certainly had gone better than I had expected, even if the phone went dead in the middle of our conversation (she doesn't recharge her phone often).

I hope that the message was delivered when she needed it most. I know my grandfather's love for my grandmother was strong, and they will be reunited when the time is right. For now, my grandfather waits for my grandmother, and, together, they will cross to the other side.

### *Message from the Spirit*
*There is no death. Only illusions of dying. Love continues without a body, because it was never contained in a body.*

# Christmas Baby

"WHERE THERE IS LOVE THERE IS LIFE."
— MAHATMA GANDHI

Our Christmas Eve party had ended, and my mother-in-law, Pam, and I stood at the sink washing the dishes while my husband and father-in-law cleaned up. The dogs were busy sniffing the floor, searching for fallen table scraps.

Pam and I talked about how wonderful the party had been, then the conversation moved to a more delicate subject—she asked how it was going with trying to have children.

Three years earlier, my husband and I decided to have a baby, and there hadn't been any reason to believe it wouldn't happen quickly, but the months, then years, went by with no results. After two-and-a-half years, I finally conceived, but by the time the blood work came back positive, I had already lost the pregnancy. Now another six months had passed and I still wasn't pregnant.

I continued washing the dishes while contemplating out loud, "It's been three years since we first tried to have a baby. It appears that we'll have to be content with our animals."

Pam stopped drying the dishes, put her hand on my shoulder, saying, "I have faith that you will have children."

Immediately I felt a bolt of energy emanate from her hand, flowing down my spine and into my womb. At that moment, I thought, "I'm pregnant!"

The next week, I bought an at-home pregnancy test and the results were positive! Nine months later, Savannah was born.

It seemed that my mother-in-law was an angel in disguise bearing the best Christmas gift of all—a baby.

## *Message from the Spirit*

*The conception was possible because of the blessing. You accepted the "right" to have a baby. The guilt you carried, because of others who could not conceive, no longer stood in your way of being the parent you wanted to be.*

# The Power of Power Animals

"Do not struggle. Go with the flow of things, and you will find yourself at one with the mysterious unity of the Universe."

— Chuang Tzu

During a shamanic healing session for a client, I was shown a herd of deer that represented her power animal. This vision was surprising because a power animal usually appears as a singular animal/bird/fish that embodies the species as an archetype energy. At the time, the herd aspect seemed interesting, but not overly important.

The next morning, the client sent me a message that her sister had emailed her an inspirational video of a deer. It was a wonderful "coincidence" that helped to confirm the healing for her.

That night after returning home late from a friend's home, I called my sister to stay awake while driving on the desolate highway. She lived out West, so while it was close to midnight in North Carolina, it was only 9:00 p.m. in Nevada. We had talked for 10 minutes when she suddenly became extremely nauseous. She said that it was odd, since she had been fine all day. She needed to end the call and we said good-bye.

A few minutes later, I drove over a hill and when I reached the top I saw a herd of deer crossing the divided highway in front of me. I looked in every direction for a path to avoid them, but there was no visible escape route. I remembered thinking, "There is no way I won't hit those deer!" I expected to hit not just one but several deer, and I surrendered to the inevitable.

Suddenly my body had a mind of its own! A presence took control of me and slammed my foot on the brakes, the screeching sound filling the night air. Time began to move in slow motion, and as I passed a deer on my left, I looked into his wide eyes that were staring back at me. He was so close that I watched the side-view mirror miss his antlers by inches. When he was safely out of the way, my hand cranked the wheel sharply to the left to dodge the deer on my right, which

kindly took several steps in the opposite direction to avoid being hit.

Now I was driving in the bumpy, grassy median and about to plow into another deer in front of me when my hand swerved the wheel back to the right, narrowly missing the doe.

Safely back on the highway, I looked in the rearview mirror to see the deer still standing there stunned. The two cars in front of me had their brakes on, no doubt wondering if they would need to stop and call 911, but when they saw me putter along the highway unharmed, their brake lights went off and everyone resumed driving.

Time returned to normal and I began to take assessment of what had just occurred. Unscathed, I first thanked God for saving the deer's lives. Then another mile down the road, I realized that I could have been killed and thanked Him for saving mine!

Although my SUV had weaved through a herd of deer while going 70 mph on the highway, I can definitively say, it was not me driving. The Spirit had taken control of my body and made all the right moves...moves I doubted even a professional race car driver could have made without divine intervention.

I saw the synchronicity of the deer power animal for my client and myself. She'd received a sign that confirmed her healing when her sister sent the video of the deer, and I encountered divine intervention when the Spirit commandeered my vehicle unharmed through a herd of deer.

When speaking with my sister the next day, I told her it was a blessing in disguise that she had gotten nauseous, otherwise I would have had a cell phone in my hand when I encountered the deer. It would have been nearly impossible to avoid hitting them with only one hand on the wheel. She replied that it was the weirdest thing, but shortly after getting off the phone, the nausea went away. Divine intervention is a wonderful thing!

### The Meaning of the Deer Power Animal

*The archetype power of the deer power animal offers many attributes, among them are the following: Manifesting for a higher good; surrendering to the Divine will; and the ability to move with intention, complete awareness and speed while remaining centered. It also represents abundance, the advent of new adventures, and the power of family or group dynamics.*

# Old Medicine Man

"You are your own judge. The verdict is up to you."

— Astrid Alauda

I was teaching a shamanic workshop one night, and the participants lay on the floor attempting their first shamanic journey. I was beating on a large buffalo drum, letting my mind lose itself to the sound vibrations when a vision began to unfold.

*I saw an old medicine man who was crying to the night sky as snow whipped around him. A blue landscape became visible, and the snow-covered tundra was littered with bodies of women, children, and men lying face down, dead and frozen to the earth like macabre sculptures. The medicine man, with his arms outstretched, blamed himself for their deaths. As their spiritual leader, he felt he should have heard the spirits' warning, and was certain he remained only to be tortured with guilt.*

When I finished drumming, the workshop participants described their shamanic journey, and I provided feedback to help them better understand what they had just experienced.

Usually I don't interrupt a workshop with details from my shamanic journeys, but the words seemed to spill out of my mouth of their own accord. As I described my vision, a participant named "Greg," who was sitting next to me, gasped. Startled, I stopped momentarily, but then continued relaying the details. When I finished, he was crying. I thought perhaps he was overly sensitive, but through his tears, Greg began to explain his reaction.

He said several other healers had told him the same story. The vision was from one of his past lives. He was the old medicine man, and he still carried the guilt from this past life, although he had been working on releasing this connection for many years.

As the workshop participants began their second journey to the beat of the drum, I was drawn back into the vision.

*The old medicine man sat on the cold ground with the snow piling around him. I asked if he was giving up. He looked at me and asked if I wouldn't do the same in his circumstance.*

*I answered that perhaps he was looking at this from the wrong perspective. He was looking at his tribe members as dead, and while his spirit had remained in this world, punishing himself over and over again, all of his people had moved on. I asked if he would like to see them.*

*We were transported to the spirit realm where the members of his tribe greeted him. They had been lovingly waiting for him.*

*I then asked him if he wanted to return to his old life, punishing himself with guilt, or stay here, reunited with*

*his tribe. He agreed to stay. And when*
*I last saw him, he was happily talking*
*to his loved ones.*

During the vision, I had heard chanting coming through the drum's vibration. It seemed the ancestors had joined us in celebration of Greg's healing. After the drumming had stopped, each participant slowly sat up, and one man looked around the room and asked, "Did anyone else hear chanting?"

"Yes!" The other participants exclaimed.

I then described the final details of the vision, and Greg listened peacefully with no tears. When I had finished, he said he also had journeyed for a healing and gained this insight: "We all choose our own destiny. Each member of my tribe had been responsible for his or her own life. It had been a misperception on my part to take responsibility for another's destiny." He had forgiven himself and felt the connection had been broken.

### Message from the Spirit

*Guilt—the universal punishment. For what? What have you done? Illusions of deeds gone wrong, misspoken words, actions that seemed to kill or harm others—all are dreams of injuries to ourselves and others, and yet they are only dreams. The spirit realm, where all the loved ones wait, is a much more accurate portrayal of yourself. Yet even this is incomplete. You are ultimately only love, extending itself for all of eternity.*

# Our Greatest Strength

"Ask not the sparrow how the eagle soars, for those with little wings have not accepted for themselves the power to share with you."

— *A Course in Miracles*

One spring morning, I looked out the window to watch the world come alive. A crow swooped. Smaller birds were chasing him. The crow rose again, dodging the smaller birds as he flew out of sight.

The scenario helped demonstrate that our greatest strength can often become a burden. The larger bird was attacked because of his size, but, unlike the crow that understood the smaller birds were afraid and attacked out of fear, most people are out of touch with their strengths.

The day before, a young man named "Steven"

had come for a healing, escorted by his father. Although still in high school, he was suffering from an undiagnosed mental illness, possibly schizophrenia or clinical depression.

He sat across from me, not understanding why he felt this way or what to do about it. I began to explain to him that I believed that people who have schizophrenia are really gifted with the ability to connect with spirits—a very powerful tool for a shaman who understands his gift and uses it wisely to connect to divine spirits, but if a person doesn't understand this gift, he can become overwhelmed by negative spirits who infiltrate his thoughts. Over time, the person becomes worn down and starts to believe that the negative thoughts are his own. The schizophrenic is like a crow that doesn't know that he is larger and stronger.

During this young man's healing, it was revealed that he was once a powerful shaman in a previous life—but a shaman who had become consumed with his own power and misused it toward the end.

The young man still held these tremendous powers, but he didn't yet realize it. The negative spirits could see his gift and were attacking him before he could remember his power and soar.

Steven's healing consisted of learning the circumstances of his past and its effects on his current life, as well as forgiveness for his previous transgressions. He was also given a message from the Spirit to be careful not to commit the same error in this lifetime.

He began to understand his life-long attraction to spiritual matters and his love of the book series, *Conversations with God*, by Neale Donald Walsch, as well as his potential to become a great spiritual leader.

The negative spirits that had attached themselves to him were removed and angels agreed to help prevent negative forces from contacting him. I spoke to him about how he would not be happy with a 9-to-5 job and needed a career that would let him express his spiritual nature to help others. He could shamanic journey or use whatever method resonated with him to connect to the divine spirits. It was now time for him to explore his power and come into his strength.

Four months later, Steven informed me that he had successfully gone off of his depression medication and was feeling noticeably better. The healing had lifted a burden that he couldn't seem to shake earlier by himself. He planned to pursue a shamanistic path.

### *Message from the Spirit*

*A distant thought emerges and you let it take the lead. You follow it back to your true self and find that the messages you had been hearing were simply distortions of the world echoing between the realities.*

# Do Not Resuscitate

"IF YOU REALIZED HOW POWERFUL YOUR THOUGHTS ARE, YOU
WOULD NEVER THINK A NEGATIVE THOUGHT."
   — PEACE PILGRIM

My mother called me to let me know that her husband, Jeff, was in the hospital. She said the nurse had just asked him if he wanted to sign a "Do Not Resuscitate" form because they did not expect him to live. Even if he did pull through, he was told he had permanent kidney damage and would need dialysis for the rest of his life. My mother said he was scared!

That afternoon, during a mini-teaching session that I was giving to a friend and my sister, I decided to shamanic journey to request a healing for my mother's husband. The spirit guide worked on his kidney, and after the healing was completed, he offered a message for Jeff. "The reason he is experiencing this illness is he doesn't want to live. As an only child, he had been very close to his parents, who both passed away in his youth. He misses them, especially his mother, and wants to be with them."

Jeff also was depressed, but the spirit guide said it was of his own doing. If he changed his attitude, he would experience a very different life. The message to Jeff was that if he wanted to live, he would. If he didn't, he would not. It was up to him.

My mother let Jeff know a healing had been performed and relayed the spirit guide's message. Now it was up to Jeff.

Two days later, my mother called and said Jeff had been released from the hospital.

"Wow!" I exclaimed, "That was quick. I guess he decided he wanted to live."

"Yes! Not only was he healed, he also is physically better than he has been in years. His sugar levels are lower and his kidney is fine. No permanent damage and no dialysis!" Later it was discovered that he no longer needed to inject insulin for his diabetes and was able to rely solely on half of an insulin pill daily. She continued, "And he is in a great mood. The depression he was in for so long is gone and now he's pleasant to be around."

A few months later when visiting my family in Michigan, I arrived at my mother's house before she did, which gave me an opportunity to speak privately with Jeff.

I asked him what the doctors had to say about his quick recovery.

"They said it was a miracle!" he answered with a big smile.

Jeff was raised in the Jewish faith, so I began to ask him questions about Judaism, such as, "How does the Jewish faith view Jesus?"

Jeff answered that Jesus was considered a prophet, then he cheerfully talked about other aspects of his religion.

Over the next few years, Jeff continued to be as active as he could, although he remained in his wheelchair due to a prior amputation.

One winter day, my mother took a day off from work to drive Jeff to the doctor to check on his diabetes. Jeff was told by the doctor he was doing well, then he and my mother spent the rest of the day running errands, including shopping at a sporting goods store in the mall to buy weights to build up Jeff's strength. At the end of the day, they ate at A&W in the food court where he had his favorite meal of French fries and a Coney dog. However, when getting back into their truck, Jeff unexpectedly didn't have the strength to get in. My mother went into the nearest store, which happened to be the sporting goods store. A store clerk came out to help her get Jeff into the vehicle, but once he was seated, he became unconscious and slumped over.

My mother called me to say she was driving Jeff to the hospital. She whispered into the phone, "I don't think he's breathing." She was only a couple of blocks from the hospital and hoped once there the medical staff would revive him.

I told her I would immediately shamanic journey for him and hung up the phone.

When I reached the spirit realm, his spirit was waiting. He began to tell me why he had died. "My body is used up...I am tired and ready to return in a new body for a new life...I miss my parents...It's too cold in Michigan...It was time." I accepted his decision.

I then asked him if he would like an aura cleansing. It was symbolic at this point and served as a ritual to help our minds adjust to his leaving this realm and moving into the next. After the cleansing, two angels lifted him up in a throne-like chair, taking him to another realm. He waved as he left, looking very happy.

When my mother called later to tell me that the hospital's efforts to revive him had failed, she said, "I guess I don't have to tell you what happened. You probably already know."

A mother's faith is a good thing. I was then able to relay his final words to her. It was comforting for her to know Jeff was content and taken care of after his passing.

During the writing of this book, I was talking with my mother and she mentioned a detail I hadn't realized. After the initial healing, five years earlier, Jeff began going to a synagogue for the first time in his adult life and attended regularly until his death. It seemed that the healing, and the love from my mother that facilitated it, had helped his spiritual journey as well.

### *Message from the Spirit*

*Your mother had a gift for restoring people to their spiritual paths—as you have experienced for yourself. Healers come in all shapes and sizes. They can be found on mountaintops or in cubicles at work. The spirit is always talking to us—sometimes it is in what we say to others and sometimes in what they say to us. Listen closely!*

# A Mother's Love is Forever

"THERE ARE NO ACCIDENTS...THERE IS ONLY SOME PURPOSE THAT WE HAVEN'T YET UNDERSTOOD."

— DEEPAK CHOPRA

I was cleaning up after a workshop that I had hosted. The sangria punch had been a hit, and I was putting the glasses in the sink when the phone rang.

I walked over to the phone, but I didn't recognize the area code and let it ring. A minute later, the phone beeped with a voice message. It was my brother asking me to call him back. Since he seldom called me, much less at 10:15 p.m., I knew it would be bad news.

I dialed the number on the caller I.D. A woman answered. I asked to speak to my brother. A moment later he answered in a wavering voice that caused my heart to sink. "Mom's been in an accident." He paused as he gathered himself. "It was really bad...she didn't make it."

How do you comprehend news that doesn't make sense? I had talked with my mother the day before, and she spoke of her plans when she retired in a few months. She recently had begun taking violin lessons and was looking forward to playing a duet with my son when we came home for Thanksgiving. She was taking acting classes and had performed in a play over the summer. When I mentioned I would be sending her the first draft of this book later that day, she squealed with delight and said she was looking forward to reading it. But now she was gone. I began to cry and after waiting a moment, my brother continued, "She was riding a bicycle when a car hit her. The officer at the scene said she was killed instantly."

This was a bad dream! My mother was so healthy that everyone believed she would outlive us all. The summer before she had built a block retaining wall in her garden by hauling blocks in a wheelbarrow and stacking them herself. Her efforts were rewarded when her garden was selected to be in the town's home garden tour.

Now all of our lives had been altered. With tears in my eyes, I told my brother I would be there the next day and hung up the phone.

I stood in the kitchen staring through the window into the night. Never had I felt so alone. I delayed walking up the stairs to tell my husband. Somehow by not repeating it, she was still alive. Finally I proceeded to our bedroom. I stood over him as he slept, tempted to let him sleep through the night, but I couldn't keep it inside any longer. I tugged on his arm until he woke up.

He turned his head and looked at me, asking, "What's wrong?"

"My mom died."

"What!?"

"She was riding a bike and was hit by a car."

I turned and walked toward the phone in my office to call my sister. She answered after a few rings.

"Sharon? Are you home?"

"Yeah, why? Is something wrong?"

I told her of mom's passing. She began to wail and scream. I waited until she finally calmed down, telling her I would see her tomorrow.

My husband and I decided to drive through the night. We picked up our kids, who were each spending the night with a friend, packed our clothes, loaded the dogs and cat in the van, and started toward Michigan after midnight.

I sobbed continuously as we drove through the night. We stopped for two hours and slept in a parking lot—checking into a hotel would have wasted too much precious time. I needed to be with my family as soon as possible.

As we drove there was a tightness in my chest that was so intense I could barely breathe. I truly did not know that grief could cause such severe physical pain.

We arrived in the afternoon, in time to eat dinner with the immediate family at my brother's home. Afterward, we felt compelled to visit our mother's house and choose what she would wear for the funeral. On the way to her house, we passed the accident scene. My brother slowed down, asking if I wanted to see it. I felt my chest tighten even more, but said, "Yes."

Florescent orange, spray-painted marks covered the road and adjacent grassy slope. Each one marked relevant evidence of the collision...a piece of a headlight here and a side-view mirror there. A circle painted around a gouge in the asphalt pavement indicated the point of impact. My brother explained the markings and finally pointed to the spot on the grassy slope where our mother had landed after being thrown from the impact. Orange letters indicated the position of her head, body and legs. How do you deal with something like this?

I crouched down and touched the grass. Anger burst forth and I thought, *Why did you leave me, mom!?*

Monday morning was a surreal dream of going to a funeral home to choose our mother's casket and plan her funeral. I kept thinking I would wake up soon and that somehow, if we all held hands and clicked our heels, things would return to normal. But the nightmare continued.

Tuesday morning, I sat on the guest bed in my in-laws' attic watching the sun filter through a window, wondering why I could feel my mother's love surrounding me like an energetic blanket radiating to the center of my soul. Her presence offered a complete immersion of love and comfort. Yet this abundance of love was strange, because when my mother was alive, I would occasionally question if she loved me at all.

I thought to myself, *Why do I know that my mother loves me now without a doubt when I wasn't sure when she was alive?*

A small voice came to me and whispered, "It's a gift."

I cried. It was a gift to feel my mother's love so perfectly. It was an indescribable comfort.

After I showered and ate lunch with my husband, we went to my mother's workplace to meet with the HR director at the state department where my mother had worked for 32 years. My sister met us there.

The HR director offered her sympathies and said that our mother's passing had a huge impact on the entire department. The State of Michigan had just offered a retirement buyout the previous week, which our mother and many others had accepted. Most set their retirement date for the end of the year. However, the HR director said two people had come into her office that morning to change their dates and retire immediately—life was too short!

She then got to the business at hand. We were told that our mother's accounts would be divided equally among her children, then the HR director mentioned that the pension would be given solely to my sister. Immediately I resented that my sister was given the entire pension, but I didn't want to feel this way!

After the meeting, we were taken to our mother's cubicle to clean it out. I was emotionally distant from my sister as we emptied the drawers. I kept battling the resentment that stabbed at me by repeatedly asking the Spirit to take this thought from me.

Suddenly my mother's spirit descended over me. Her presence completely surrounded me and her vision became mine. Through her eyes, the whole world glowed with love while beams of light radiated from my sister. My mother's memories filled my consciousness, and I could see my sister as the little girl, the teenager, and the young woman she had raised. My mother saw her as an innocent daughter, who would be taken care of with the pension she had inherited. I felt the comfort that it gave my mother and the love she had for my sister. Immediately all resentment left me. I knew my mother had given the pension out of love, and as I experienced that love, it became impossible for me to feel anything else.

Then my mother was gone.

I realized that my mother had sent me two beautiful gifts after her passing. First, she comforted me with the knowledge of her undying love, then she immersed her spirit with mine, and, for a brief moment, I saw my sister through her vision of all-encompassing love, which healed my heart.

Love is perfect and never dies. My mother reminded me of this basic truth.

### Message from the Spirit

*Your mother's love came when you needed it most. She thought only of her love for her children, family and friends. She highly regarded her life, accomplishments, and even things left undone.*

*Things left undone seem to be the hardest part of letting go...yet those were the lessons that did not need to be learned. Look at those as accomplishments.*

# The Art of Love

"If you hear a voice within you say 'you cannot paint,' then by all means paint, and that voice will be silenced."
— Vincent Van Gogh

It was a cold, rainy night when we entered the old country church. My family was there to meet with the pastor and discuss the details of our mother's funeral service.

We walked past the sanctuary and down a hallway lined with paintings on the walls. Some of the artwork looked familiar and I paused to search for the artist's signature. In the lower corner was the name I had expected..."Eva". As I faced planning the funeral service for my mother—the most important woman in my life—I thought how odd that these paintings should remind me of yet another woman who helped shape my life.

Eva was a well-known art teacher in my hometown. She lived on a farm on the outskirts of Mason and taught lessons in a sunroom with a scenic view of the cornfields.

I first met Eva when I was 12. One of my school friends, who didn't want to take art lessons alone, had begged me to join her. My friend went a few times, but I continued taking lessons from Eva until I graduated from high school.

Over the years, Eva became my confidant, in addition to being a wonderful art teacher. She was one of the few nonjudgmental adults in my life. I would talk about problems at school or home while I painted, and she would stand next to me with a pleasant smile on her face, patiently listening to my teenage woes. She also encouraged me to submit my paintings into art shows and the county fair—we were both thrilled when I won "Best of Show".

At the end of my senior year, her art guild awarded me a two-week stay at the Blue Lake Fine Arts Camp. It was a wonderful honor for me, and I am sure it cost Eva and the art guild more than I ever paid for my art lessons.

We stayed in touch over the years, and when her

husband passed away, my mother and I went to his funeral visitation. Eva was so happy to see us, and held my hand as we talked about her husband's kind ways and love of black licorice.

The years went by and one October she died. Unfortunately I did not hear of her passing until a few months later.

I sent a letter to her residence inquiring about where she was buried and hoped for a reply, so I could visit her gravesite. A letter soon arrived from her grandson with a funeral service card and a short note, indicating she had been buried in the Eaton Rapids Cemetery.

Previously I had visited the small city of Eaton Rapids to eat at a popular, old-fashioned ice cream parlor, and on another occasion, my mother and I went to an art gallery to meet a featured artist. It was also where an old boyfriend of mine had grown up, and, on several occasions, he and I had driven through the historic downtown, past a picturesque cemetery, to visit his parents who lived just outside the city.

That night I had a vivid dream that I was driving to visit Eva's gravesite when I saw my old boyfriend standing on a grassy hilltop. I pulled off the road, got out of the car, and walked up the hill to where he was standing. He had prepared a picnic and invited me to join him. I sat down and told him that I was on my way to visit Eva's gravesite in the cemetery near his parent's house. But as the conversation continued, I found his eagerness and nasally voice irritating, and became anxious to get going. I said good-bye and started walking down the hill, then the dream ended.

The next day, on a bitter-cold January afternoon, I set out to pay my respects to Eva. Following the route that I had taken with my old boyfriend, I drove into Eaton Rapids, took a left on the main street, and then slowed down as I got near where I expected the cemetery to be. But there was no cemetery in sight, instead, the road was lined with houses. How strange. Cemeteries don't just disappear!

I drove back and forth several times, certain it should be there. Nothing.

Exasperated, I stopped at the corner store and asked the clerk if she knew where the cemetery was.

She glanced out the storefront window and said, "It's over there."

I looked out the window, but only saw the busy street and houses. I turned back to her and said, "I don't see it."

"Well, take that side street there," she said, pointing to it. "Go several blocks, then take a right. You can't miss it."

I followed the clerk's directions and pulled up to the entrance of the Rose Hill Cemetery—which was not the name Eva's grandson had indicated in his letter.

Several things became obvious to me at this point. First, the cemetery had never been visible from the main street, and second, if I had tried to look up the address of the cemetery with the name that Eva's grandson had given me, I wouldn't have found it. I began to understand that my old memories of the cemetery were not based on actual sightings, but rather on visions, so that today, I could find the cemetery where Eva was buried.

I entered the grounds and was immediately faced with crisscrossing, snow-covered roads and gravesites as far as the eye could see. Since Eaton Rapids is a small town, I had thought it would be easy to find Eva's gravesite, but now I feared I might not be able to find it at all.

Eva's grandson had indicated she was buried in the far right corner. I drove straight ahead and took the third right, making my way over the crackling snow when I saw a tombstone with the name "Saper" on it. I braked. There was only one family in this city with that surname—my old boyfriend's! A fact he'd proudly mentioned many times while we were dating.

As I read the inscription, I was saddened to learn his father, "George Saper," had died and wished him a peaceful journey. I turned away and started to drive forward when I saw Eva's tombstone through the windshield. Stunned, I looked back to Saper's tombstone and once again to Eva's—astonished that the tombstone of my old boyfriend's father would be within eyesight of Eva's. It became clear why my old boyfriend had been in my dream—the Spirit had used his presence as a beacon to lead me to Eva's gravesite.

I pulled the car closer to her gravesite and got out. The winter wind was harsh and I tightened my coat hood. And as I stood before Eva's tombstone, I remembered all that she had done for me and offered my gratitude for the love, encouragement and friendship she had given me.

### Message from the Spirit

*Sometimes the teacher is the student, and the student is the teacher. We all have much to learn from each other. Live wisely, give freely. Kindness means so much.*

# The Lost Diamond

"IN SEARCH OF MY MOTHER'S GARDEN, I FOUND MY OWN."
  — ALICE WALKER

A slight scratch on my finger alerted me to the fact that an accent diamond had fallen out of my wedding ring. Although relatively inexpensive to replace, I became dismayed and wondered if it was an omen.

All of my life, I have been a "finder" of things. Once, when I lost one of my earrings in a snow bank, I tediously searched until I found the small, gold hoop that had been a gift from my grandmother. She had bought the earrings during a trip to Mexico. I remembered opening the gift box in front of my parents and relatives, so proud to receive my first pair of gold earrings. It was a rite of passage for an Hispanic girl at the tender age of five.

I now hoped to find the small, yet sentimental, diamond and began searching the entire house. I ran my hand over the carpet in my office and bedroom, inspected the shower, put my head on the tile floors for an eye-level view, patted the bed sheets, and peered into crevices of my computer keyboard. Finally after an hour of searching, I gave up.

I sat down on the floor and pulled my mother's purse onto my lap. It had been a month since her unexpected death. Her purse was full of lotions, lipstick, papers, reward cards, address sheets, and all those little bits that comprised her everyday life. I unzipped a small pocket where her wedding ring had been placed for safekeeping. Holding it in my hands, I thought about how she was gone, but her ring was intact—and yet, I was still alive, although my wedding ring was in disrepair. Was this irony or simply me overreacting due to her recent passing?

I decided I was torturing myself and put the ring back in the pocket, setting the purse on the shelf to wait for another day when I would browse through it once more to feel my mother's presence.

Normally I would not get this upset over losing an item, but the lost diamond was part of my wedding ring, which symbolized another very important relationship in my life. I felt that I was losing everything—although I knew this wasn't true.

I stood up and admitted to myself that I could not find the diamond, but then a vision of a vacuum cleaner sucking it up went through my mind. I needed to find the diamond soon or it would be lost forever. I decided to ask for the Spirit's help and said this simple prayer, "Please help me find the lost diamond. I can't do it on my own."

I then released the outcome to the Spirit and walked into my home office to proof the laser prints of this book. When I discovered that the pages had printed in the wrong order, I said a few choice words and momentarily let my peace leave me. However, I quickly gathered myself and began to patiently take each page and put it in the correct sequence. Halfway through the stack, I heard a quiet voice say, "Look down. It's there."

I looked at the carpet and caught a faint glimmer. Reaching down, I picked up a tiny, clear fragment to take a closer look. It was the missing diamond! I said a prayer of thanks and was amazed, yet again, at how the Spirit hears our prayers—no matter how big or small.

The following Monday, I took my wedding ring to a jeweler to have the diamond reset. I handed the sales clerk my ring and the loose diamond taped to the inside of a plastic baggy. She took a closer look at the small accent diamond and exclaimed, "It's a miracle you found it!"

A smile grew on my face as I appreciated her affirmation of the miracle, but I realized that the most important aspect of finding the lost diamond had been the recognition that I am learning to rely on the Spirit's guidance and hear Its voice more clearly as each day passes.

### Message from the Spirit

*Rewards come in all sizes, but ultimately they are all the same measure. The power source is consistent. It is only your listening that varies.*

# Conclusion

I was in the spirit realm to perform a healing for a client when I saw my mother's spirit waiting for me. She had passed away a little over a month ago and was now sitting next to a fire roasting marshmallows. I walked over and sat down to join her. I joked that she was always eating, but she ignored my jab and handed me the hot marshmallow. I ate the gooey treat while I talked about what the kids and I had been up to, then I told her it was time to perform my client's healing and left with my power animal.

When I returned from the healing, the fire was smoldering and my mother was gone. Saddened, I lay by my power animal for comfort. He recommended that we visit the garden behind us, which represents the state of my spiritual well being. If it's lush and free from weeds, I know my spirit's growth is progressing nicely. If I find a plant that is dying, I know there is an issue to which I must tend.

My power animal and I walked through the wrought-iron gates that gave the garden a stately feel. Inside, I was surprised to find my mother weeding the garden. She stood up and smiled when she saw me. She wore old work clothes that were covered with dirt and held weeds in each hand.

"Mom, what are you doing working in my garden?" I asked.

"Just helping out," she answered.

Indeed, gardening had been her passion in life, yet this scene was also symbolic of how she had helped many people find their spiritual path during her lifetime.

An angel wrapped his arm around her and said how special she was. I recognized that his statement was a compliment and a joke, since we are all special.

As I stood in the garden watching the golden light surround her, I realized that my mother had always been tending to my spiritual garden.

# About the Author

Elizabeth M. Herrera is a shamanic healer and author of life-changing books. Her stories encourage people to stretch outside their comfort zones and reexamine their own beliefs.

She inherited her rebellious spirit from her father who was raised by his grandfather—a full-blooded Apache who smuggled sugar and flour from Mexico into Texas, exchanged gunfire with Texas Rangers and crossed paths with Pancho Villa.

Elizabeth was raised in a Christian home, but lost her faith in her early twenties. For over a decade, she searched for something to fill the void, eventually discovering Native American spirituality (shamanism). Through this spiritual practice, she unexpectedly became a catalyst for healing and miracles. These events led her back to a belief in a higher power.

Always drawn to the spiritual side of life,

Elizabeth began her shamanic path in Michigan where she learned to shamanic journey with Stephanie Tighe (a certified Sandra Ingerman instructor). Elizabeth continued her studies through the Foundation for Shamanic Studies for shamanic journeying, soul retrieval, and death and dying (psychopomp), but her major source of learning has been from her spirit guides, who offer limitless guidance and lessons on living a more spiritual life. To learn more, visit her healing website at ShamanElizabeth.com.

Elizabeth is the author of *Earth Sentinels: The Storm Creators* (Contemporary Fantasy), *Of Stars and Clay* (Fantasy, Science Fiction, Dystopian), and *Dreams of Heaven* (Spiritual Fiction).

# Overview of Shamanism and Shamanic Journeying

Shamanism is the oldest known spiritual practice in the world and is still practiced by indigenous people on every continent today. While there are many different rituals, one commonality is that the shaman acts as a catalyst between this world and the spirit world.

Sandra Ingerman and Hank Wesselman, in the book, *Awakening to the Spirit World,* offered this insight: "Shamanism is an ancient and powerful spiritual practice that can help us thrive during challenging and changing times. In our modern-day technological world we have been led to believe that what we see, touch, hear, smell, and taste with our ordinary senses connects us only to the world that is visible around us. Conversely, shamanism teaches that there are doorways into other realms of reality where helping spirits reside who can share guidance, insight, and healing not just for ourselves but also for the world in which we live."

I personally have found the practice of shamanism to be life changing. The connection to the Divine power has opened my mind to the wonders of the unseen world, which affects every aspect of our lives and even the entire universe. Through shamanism, I have learned that we are all connected—the earth, sky, nature, animals, winged and sea creatures, and mankind—singing one song of unending love.

Here is a short overview of shamanic journeying:

~ During a shamanic journey, a shaman will use a visionary process to travel to the spirit realm to request healings, receive divine messages, help guide lost souls home (psychopomp), and commune with nature and the universe.

~ In the spirit realm, a shaman interacts with spirit guides, ancestors, spirits of people from this world, angels, and enlightened beings.

~ Power animals act as protectors and guides for the shaman. They can be a part of a shaman's journeys for many lifetimes or brief periods during which their archetype power is needed.

~ The spirit realm has three "worlds": the lower, middle, and upper. None of the realms are better than the others; they simply offer different experiences that are appropriate for different circumstances.

41311789R00095

Made in the USA
San Bernardino, CA
02 July 2019